"You remind me of a horse I once owned."

J.D. rested one booted foot on the bumper of his truck.

"Is that all you can talk about? Horses?" Deanna was surprised to find herself feeling slightly insulted.

J.D. ignored her. "She was a beautiful thing," he remembered. "But she was also the most contrary mare I ever had the misfortune to ride. I can't tell you how many times I ended up on my backside in the dirt."

Deanna smiled at the image, then scowled as a thought struck her. "What happened to her? Did you get rid of her?"

"No. You see—" he gave her a slow, sensuous smile "—I like my females spirited."

As the full meaning of his words sunk in, Deanna blushed. "Save your breath, Mr. Vaughn. The old 'spirited filly' line is not only cliched, it's also insulting. Your poor attempts at flattery won't get you my horse."

Dear Reader,

The American Southwest is one of the last domains of the wild mustang herds that roamed the United States a century ago. But even this area is dwindling, due to the ever-increasing encroachments of man.

The Adopt-A-Horse organization referred to in my story really does exist. Our limited land preserves can support only so many mustangs, since grazing sites and water are at a premium in rugged mountain country. Surplus animals are rounded up by Adopt-A-Horse, checked by vets and adopted out for nominal fees.

It takes a very special kind of person to make a commitment to such untamed creatures and to gain their trust. I met people like this at the Arizona stables where I boarded my own horses. Animal lovers such as my husband, Roger, and our friends Ray and Tawnee spent hours of their free time healing and training not only mustangs but domestic horses who were cast off and abused in today's throwaway society. My own mare, Lightning Bug, was a lame, gashed, skeletal victim of neglect before my husband and I took her in. She went from being a potential slaughterhouse candidate to a healthy, contented animal who repaid us with many hours of pleasure. The rambling rides I took on Buggy through the desert were such a contrast to what her fate could have been!

On the Line is dedicated to all those who believe that the great American wilderness should *remain* great. The finest gift we can leave our children is the beauty of our land, and the proud, wild creatures who inhabit it.

Sincerely,

Anne Marie Duquette

ON THE LINE
Anne Marie Duquette

Harlequin Books

TORONTO • NEW YORK • LONDON
AMSTERDAM • PARIS • SYDNEY • HAMBURG
STOCKHOLM • ATHENS • TOKYO • MILAN
MADRID • WARSAW • BUDAPEST • AUCKLAND

ISBN 0-373-03289-7

ON THE LINE

CHAPTER ONE

"IT'S *HIM* AGAIN."

"Again?" Deanna Leighton, D.V.M., pushed straggly black curls out of her face. "That's the fifth time he's called this morning!"

"Shall I tell him you're busy?"

"You've told him that, Mom. Just like you told him we've been unexpectedly swamped with patients."

Deanna glanced around with dismay at the animal-and-owner pairs crowded into the waiting room of her veterinary office. Thanks to a virulent strain of canine flu, everyone and his dog was there. And there were more patients outside. Sighing, she peered out the window at the trailers holding horses that needed to be checked, as well. If she didn't know better, she'd swear the entire animal population of tiny Cactus Gulch, Arizona, was here.

Her mother and office manager, Helen Leighton, looked at Deanna for guidance. "So what do you want me to say?" she asked in a whisper.

"I'll take it." Deanna gestured for the phone. "And this time, I'm not going to be polite. *What?*" she said harshly.

"Dr. Leighton?" queried a deep, husky voice.

"This is Dr. Leighton. The same Dr. Leighton who has a roomful of patients. My secretary has repeatedly explained that I can't talk to you today, Mr. Vaughn."

"Please, call me J.D. And this won't take long. I want to discuss buying your horse. I'm only asking for five minutes, Doctor. You and your barracuda of a secretary have wasted more time than that hanging up on me," came the blunt retort.

"Barracuda!" Deanna's dark brown eyes fired with outrage. "That *barracuda* is my mother!"

A pause. Then, "I'm sorry, I didn't mean—"

"Save it, Mr. Vaughn." Deanna's voice grew louder and louder, and the noise in the waiting room grew quieter and quieter. "I wouldn't sell you the shovel I muck out my horse's stall with, let alone a living, breathing animal. If you dare to interrupt my work again, I swear I'll —"

"Deanna, sweetheart ..."

Deanna looked up at her mother's anxious warning. She suddenly realized that everyone was eavesdropping on the conversation. Her cheeks flushed a bright red.

"Goodbye, Mr. Vaughn." She slammed down the receiver with an equal mixture of fury and embarrassment.

"Send in the next patient, please," she said with as much dignity as she could muster. "I'll be in my office."

But it wasn't the next patient who entered her office. It was Helen herself.

"Deanna, are you okay?" her mother asked. She sat down and studied her daughter anxiously. "It isn't like you to lose your temper—at least not in the office."

Helen, a Hispanic American, had always lived in Arizona, while her late husband Carl had been from back East. Although Deanna took after her mother in looks, she'd inherited neither of her parents' calm demeanors. Being harassed by phone calls at her small practice on an unusually busy Monday morning didn't help.

"I know, Mom, but he makes me so mad! I've told him a million times I don't want to sell my horse."

"Mr. Vaughn's offered you a lot of money. Money you could certainly use."

Deanna vigorously shook her head. "Rustler's a pet. I don't sell pets, no matter how much cash I'm offered."

"But Deanna, your horse isn't an ordinary pet," Helen reminded her. "He's a prime stallion with champion bloodlines and the papers to prove it. And J. D. Vaughn is a horse breeder and racer. It's only logical he'd be interested."

"He's a *quarter-horse* breeder, Mom. Rustler's a *Thoroughbred*."

Helen sighed. "Yes, but Mr. Vaughn wants to branch out. Thoroughbred racing's been his goal ever since he started breeding quarter horses seven years ago."

"So he's said during his numerous phone calls," Deanna grumbled, but Helen continued.

"His quarter horses are very successful. So is the single Thoroughbred mare he has racing. The other local breeders won't sell him a Thoroughbred stallion for breeding because they consider him a threat. They've all banded together against him."

"That's his problem, not mine." Deanna was merciless. "I was the one who found Rustler. I was the one who rescued him from that animal-adoption agency and spent months nursing him back to health." The memory still made Deanna furious. "Rustler was so skinny. I could count every rib!"

"I remember. I was there too, Deanna," her mother said softly.

Deanna crossed her arms. "Then you should understand why under *no* circumstances will I sell my horse to a coldhearted businessman who's trying to increase his bank account. J. D. Vaughn only wants Rustler for his earning potential."

"I'm not telling you to sell your horse! But this is a small town, and secrets are hard to keep in small towns. You're going to have to deal with this sooner or later. It didn't take Mr. Vaughn long to find out about Rustler. Others will, too."

Deanna's heart sank. She hadn't considered that possibility when she'd first become involved in reporting and prosecuting an animal abuser, then had impulsively adopted the man's horse from the local humane society. It was hard enough to believe that anyone could cruelly abuse then discard an animal—let alone such a valuable one. So when the humane society had sent Rustler's overlooked registration papers to Deanna weeks after she'd acquired the horse, she'd been astounded.

"You're going to have to try to see things from Mr. Vaughn's perspective."

Deanna froze. "*His* perspective? How can you even suggest such a thing? Seven years ago Dad spent every cent we had on a Thoroughbred racehorse that J. D. Vaughn sold to him, trained for him and raced for him! Mother, we lost our ranch, our house, our savings, everything!"

Deanna choked on the words. Unfortunately, J. D. Vaughn's early attempts at Thoroughbred racing were not nearly as successful as his early quarter-horse attempts. Seven years ago he'd been forced to abandon the former, and Carl Leighton had been one of the casualties.

"If I hadn't gotten a scholarship to college, I'd be slinging hash at some diner! And look at you!"

Deanna sadly took in the wrinkles on Helen's face and the thick streaks of gray in hair that had once been as black as her own.

"You haven't had a new dress in two years because Dad didn't leave you anything. You answer phones and type all day long, then at night you help me scrub the surgery and the animal pens. My own mother! What kind of a life is that?"

Deanna's voice choked as she remembered the numerous times Helen had refused to let Deanna handle the messy cleanups alone. It was an ongoing battle between the pair, one Deanna always lost. Helen could be just as stubborn as Deanna when she chose.

"I don't mind," Helen insisted.

"Well, I do! You should be retired and enjoying life, not working crazy hours and living in a rented place with me! Thanks to Dad and all the debts he left, I can't even afford to pay you a decent salary," Deanna said with fury and shame.

"Or yourself," Helen gently reminded her. "Deanna, I like working with you. I really, truly enjoy my job. Even the dirtier aspects of it don't bother me. But what *does* bother me is how much your father's death has affected you. Carl died six years ago, yet you're still so bitter. Can't you forgive him? I have."

Deanna gazed at her mother, seeing her old worn clothes and thinking about their shabby office with its stained walls and peeling linoleum. A hard look came into her eyes.

"I know you loved him, Deanna," Helen added. "We both did."

"Yes, I loved him. But I hate what he did to you. To *us.* J. D. Vaughn was a big part of that. The last thing I need is a *second* business deal with the man who helped ruin my father and left us dead broke."

"Then you shouldn't have rescued a dying horse with impeccable bloodlines."

"But, Mom, I honestly didn't know! Those registration papers came weeks after I took Rustler in. I never guessed someone else would want him—especially J. D. Vaughn! I certainly never imagined you'd want to let that man back in our lives."

Helen stood up stiffly. "If you intend to keep your horse, you're going to have to deal with Mr. Vaughn—and any other breeder who comes along."

As Deanna watched her mother walk back to the front desk, she rubbed her temples with shaking hands. Carl Leighton hadn't just left a huge debt behind; his death had driven a wedge into what had once been a peaceful mother-and-daughter relationship.

That realization, and the onset of a headache, heralded a terrible morning for Deanna. The owners, who were as difficult as their flu-stricken pets, continued to show up nonstop, forcing Helen and Deanna to skip lunch. Ordinarily the two of them could easily handle the patient load, but an onslaught like today's overtaxed them both.

And just when Deanna thought matters couldn't get any worse, J. D. Vaughn phoned again and announced he was on his way over.

"Forget it! I'm not selling my— Hello? Hello? Doesn't that man ever take no for an answer?" Deanna muttered.

"Obviously not. Your next case is out back in the holding pen. He needs to be stitched."

"Please let it not be—"

"Mrs. Foley's bad-tempered gelding? The one who keeps charging into the barbed-wire fence? It is."

Deanna groaned at the thought of one of her most regular and least desired customers. The horse's foul temper was surpassed only by his elderly owner's.

"I'd put your steel-toed boots on," Helen suggested calmly. "They're in your office. I have your equine kit right here. Be careful, dear."

"Be careful, she tells me," Deanna grumbled as she took off the grubby white smock that covered her usual working outfit of jeans and a plaid shirt. "As if I'd turn my back on *that* beast." She kicked off well-worn cowboy boots and replaced them with lace-up steel-toed ones.

Deanna looked at the wall clock, scowling at the lateness of the hour and resenting every second she wasted on tying up the boots. There was still a waiting room full of patients to see, but Mrs. Foley's gelding had inflicted more than one broken toe on the unwary. She'd just finished with the second boot when the screaming started.

"What in the world?" Deanna raced to the window. "Oh, no!"

Mrs. Foley's gelding was no longer in the back holding pen. He was in the dirt parking lot among the cars, kicking and bucking like a prize rodeo bronco. Mrs. Foley was trying to grab the horse's bridle, but her angry shrieks only agitated the horse further.

"Mom! My rope!" Deanna yelled, but her ever-efficient mother had already retrieved it from the equine kit and tossed it to her.

Deanna dashed outside. "Mrs. Foley, please be quiet!" she hissed, uncoiling the rope. "If you keep this up, your horse will never calm down!"

As if for emphasis, the gelding lashed out with a rear hoof, squarely hitting someone's car door and leaving a good-size dent.

"If he runs away, I'll never catch him. Do something!" Mrs. Foley wailed, clutching Deanna's arm.

"I can't slip this noose over his head if you don't let go of me!" Deanna pulled away from Mrs. Foley, her eyes on the nervous shifting hoofs. "Now get out of the way and let me try to rope him."

Deanna slowly walked up to the horse, who immediately shied away. Only the ring of cars kept him from bolting.

"Have you ever thought about getting a new horse?" Deanna said as the horse again eluded her. "This one's too big a handful for you."

"I couldn't. He's my baby." Mrs. Foley wrung her hands, then dodged behind a car as the gelding charged.

Deanna jumped to the side, threw the noose—and missed. Then she, too, was ducking behind a car for safety. She took a deep breath and was starting to straighten up when a hand under her elbow startled her.

"What?" She turned and looked up into a pair of deep blue eyes.

"Let me have the rope."

His commanding tone made Deanna blink. "Who are you?" she asked, taking in his tanned face, thick brown hair and strong chin.

"Someone with good aim—courtesy of the rodeo circuit."

Deanna stared at him in disbelief. His tailored silk shirt and linen blazer screamed high fashion. He *was* wearing jeans and boots, but they weren't the serviceable kind. No bronco-riding rodeo cowboy she knew would ever wear designer jeans and a turquoise-inlaid belt buckle, let alone risk those expensive intricately tooled boots around wild bulls.

"I can help," he insisted.

Deanna forced herself to be polite. "Of course you can. But this horse is my patient, and I'm responsible for him."

The man's eyes sparked with annoyance, but when he spoke it was with easy humor. "You're either quite capable—or quite patronizing. Which is it?"

"I've done this before. This horse is one of my worst patients, not to mention one of the best escape artists I've ever seen."

The man smiled. "Really?" he drawled. "I do love a challenge."

Deanna shook her head. "You wouldn't stand a chance."

His smile grew. A most attractive smile, Deanna noticed.

"I suppose I'll have to prove it to you." He shrugged off the blazer and carelessly tossed it across a dusty car hood. Deanna cringed at his disregard for the costly fabric. Next he unbuttoned the sleeves of the silk shirt before shoving them above his elbows.

"Give me the rope."

Deanna stared with amazement at his muscled forearms and the width of his shoulders and chest. She'd been around working men far too long not to recognize the truth. Despite his appearance, this man was no inexperienced dandy. Suddenly, strangely, the look in his eyes inspired confidence.

After a moment's hesitation, she passed the rope to him. "Be careful," she warned. "That is one mean horse."

The gelding pawed at the ground, then let go with another flying kick. This one hit a brand-new pickup, leaving a deep gouge in the side. Deanna winced, glad that Mrs. Foley would—as she had numerous times before—pay for any damage her horse inflicted.

"I hope that truck wasn't yours," Deanna said.

"Nope."

Deanna watched as the man stood up and hefted the rope in his hand, checking its weight. He frowned at the noose Deanna had made, then shook out a lariat-size loop.

"You aren't going to hurt him, are you?" Mrs. Foley called. "I'll have you know my husband's a lawyer, and if you so much as..."

The man threw Mrs. Foley a hard look, and, to Deanna's amazement, the older woman immediately shut up.

"I wish I could do that!" Deanna marveled under her breath.

The quick grin the man gave Deanna had her pulse racing. Then, just as quickly, the rope sailed through the air and settled around the horse's neck.

"Well done!" Deanna clapped her hands as the man effortlessly reeled in the horse. Even Mrs. Foley was impressed, judging by the sudden slackness of her jaw.

"He's got a bad cut here," the man said as the horse nervously skittered about. "Barbed wire?"

"Yes. I was about to sew it up when he escaped from the back pen."

"I'll hold him while you take care of it. Where's your twitch?" he asked, referring to the small portable nose clamp used to control an unruly horse, the same way a nose ring was used to control a savage bull.

"Right here." Deanna reached into her pocket. "I've got to run inside and get my kit, but I'll be right back. Thank you, Mr. . . ."

"Vaughn."

Deanna's hand froze in the process of giving him the twitch. "Vaughn? As in J. D. Vaughn?" Despite all the grief the man had caused her family, Deanna had never met him before. If he wasn't off racing his quarter horses, he'd been at out-of-town auctions seeking new prospects.

"At your service, ma'am."

Deanna's blood boiled at his smug, purely masculine look. She left to get her equine kit with a stiff angry back, and her anger was still rising when she returned to his side. Thanks to J. D. Vaughn, the gelding behaved beautifully while she stitched him up. To her disgust, the patient further cooperated by calmly allowing J.D. to lead him back into Mrs. Foley's horse trailer.

Her blood pressure peaked when J.D. followed her inside and was greeted with applause from everyone who'd watched from the big front window.

"Nice work, young feller," praised one elderly gentleman with an ailing German shepherd. "I could use you with my cattle."

"Thanks, but I had enough of cattle on my parents' ranch," J.D. said. He brushed at the dirt on his blazer just once, then slung it over his shoulder. The pose didn't seem deliberate, but it was definitely effective.

Deanna rolled her eyes as all the younger women—and some of the older—openly admired the newcomer. Unfortunately she had to admit that J.D.'s presence added a certain excitement to her dreary waiting room.

"You aren't a cattleman?" the dog owner persisted.

"Used to be. I'm into quarter horses now. And Thoroughbreds," he said with a pointed look at Deanna.

"Perhaps we can talk about that later," Deanna said grudgingly. "I'm sorry, but as you can see..." She gestured toward her waiting patients.

"You look like you could use a hand or two. And I've got a spare pair right here." He tossed his jacket over the counter that separated Helen's work area from the waiting-room chairs, then gave Helen a big smile. "You wouldn't hold a thoughtless remark against me, would you, Mrs. Leighton? You're the prettiest barracuda I've ever seen, and I'm sorry my temper got the best of me."

Deanna fumed as her mother actually returned the enemy's smile. "It's okay, Mr. Vaughn. I know all about people with tempers." Helen gave Deanna an amused glance. "And we could use your help. This is the busiest we've been since Deanna graduated and started practicing two years ago."

"Mother! I can handle things myself!"

"The man's obviously been around animals," Helen said logically. "Besides, we've already missed our lunch. I'd prefer not to miss dinner, as well."

Deanna looked from her mother's face to J. D. Vaughn's, then once again at the crowded waiting room. She had no choice.

"All right, Mr. Vaughn," she said in an undertone meant for his ears only. "But our personal business can wait. I don't want to hear one single word about Thoroughbreds until the last patient goes home. And in front of the pet owners you'll address me as Dr. Leighton and my mother as Mrs. Leighton. Is that understood?"

"Yes, ma'am." The man slung his thumbs through his belt loops, causing a few more sighs from the women in the waiting room.

"And for heaven's sake, stop posing," Deanna grumbled, "or we'll never get out of here."

"Deanna!" Helen scolded, but twenty-eight-year-old Dr. Deanna Leighton was no schoolgirl. She ignored mother's rare censure. Instead, she glared at the culprit responsible for her troubles.

"Please send in the next patient," she said to her mother. She then swept regally out of the waiting room, but not before she heard Helen join the enemy camp.

"Don't mind her, Mr. Vaughn. I know you weren't posing, even if Deanna doesn't."

"No, but it certainly got your lovely daughter's attention. I might have to do it more often," was his insufferable reply.

Then the two of them were laughing together, along with a few eavesdropping pet owners. A seething Deanna wasn't sure how she was going to get through the afternoon in one piece.

Somehow she managed. J.D.'s gentle hands, soothing voice and firm strength kept more than one unruly pet or owner in line. Deanna studiously avoided talking to J.D., but it wasn't really that hard, since her clients' incessant chatter nicely prevented it. Apparently J. D. Vaughn was more than just a successful horse racer; he was actually an ex-rodeo star. One quite well-known to many of her older patrons, and they had no shame when it came to questioning him.

Deanna found herself carefully paying attention to every comment, strictly for strategic reasons, she told herself.

"I remember you took the national bronc-riding championship four years in a row, J.D.," one admirer remembered while Deanna doctored his cat. "Only you went by 'Dallas' Vaughn then, right?"

"Right," he replied. "Dallas is my middle name."

"You're from Dallas?" the other man asked.

"No, Colorado. But my parents were there on a stock-buying trip when I was— Well, let's just say they mixed business with pleasure." His eyes met Deanna's and twinkled wickedly. She looked away. "My first name's Jonathan."

"Jon Vaughn isn't exactly a bronc rider's name."

"That's why I used Dallas when I worked the rodeo circuit. But my friends have always called me J.D."

The fan nodded. "Why'd you quit? You were on top and winning big."

"I was twenty-three. I'd been on the rodeo circuit since I was seventeen and was more than ready to walk away— preferably with all my bones intact," J.D. replied as Deanna wrapped the injured tabby's hind leg. "Besides, I'd done what I'd set out to do."

"And what was that?" Deanna's question slipped out despite her resolve to be indifferent.

J.D. continued to hold the cat, but his gaze never left her face. "I wanted to get away from cattle ranching and into horse breeding. But horse breeding and racing aren't cheap. Riding in rodeos provided money for my degree in equine studies, then later, seed money for my quarter-horse ranch."

Deanna's eyes opened wide. "You must have been very good," she said, doing some quick mental calculations. She knew he'd been in the racing business for seven years. If he'd graduated four years after he left the rodeo circuit, that made him thirty-four.

"Oh, he was, Doc," said the cat owner. "And not just with the broncos. He won the calf-roping championship two years in a row, or was it three?"

"Three," J.D. confirmed. Deanna finished with the cat, and J.D. carefully lifted the animal and placed him in his owner's arms.

"And you won a bull-riding title, right?"

"Now that was a fluke," J.D. said matter-of-factly. "I rarely rode bulls, but all the big-name riders were injured that year. I took a chance, and it paid off. That was the last win I needed to retire and buy the Rocking J. Have you heard of it?" he asked Deanna curiously.

Oh, she'd definitely heard of it. Her father had lost every cent he owned—and more. Deanna couldn't believe the irony. J. D. Vaughn was back in her life, as if her first encounter with him hadn't been bad enough.

"The Rocking J Ranch provides some of the best racing quarter horses in Arizona," the cat owner told Deanna admiringly when she didn't answer. "It's only an hour or so drive from here."

"I don't follow racing," Deanna stated coldly, then changed the subject to the cat's care.

J.D. gave her an assessing look, but said nothing. And for the rest of the long afternoon, Deanna carefully avoided joining in on any conversation concerning J. D. Vaughn.

Finally the last patient had gone, and only Deanna, Helen and J.D. remained. Helen was busy closing out the books for the day, while Deanna was tallying the total on the drug cabinet. When she was done, she locked the cabinet, took off her soiled smock and threw it into the laundry hamper.

J.D. looked around. "What can I do to help?"

"Not a thing," Helen replied before Deanna could answer. "We don't have any overnight patients to feed, and I'm almost finished with the billing. You and Deanna are free to go."

"Mom, I'm not going to leave you with the cleanup," Deanna protested. "Don't you dare touch a thing without me!"

"I won't. We'll do it tonight. We've been going nonstop since breakfast. You need to eat, and so do I."

"I'll buy," J.D. immediately volunteered.

Deanna started to say he would not, but her mother interrupted. "Thank you, but I'm tired, and I'd prefer a *quiet* dinner," Helen emphasized. "You and Deanna go. Deanna, please leave me the truck. Mr. Vaughn can take you home after dinner."

Deanna would have argued, but J.D. had opened the front door and was holding it for her. Deanna scowled at her mother, then stepped through. J. D. Vaughn was close behind.

"My car's over here," he said. "Let me get the door for you."

Deanna glanced at his car, then shook her head. "No."

"No?"

She had the satisfaction of seeing his eyes narrow in annoyance. "You're not buying me dinner, Mr. Vaughn, any more than you're buying my horse. So you can save yourself the cost of a meal."

She placed her hands on her hips and issued a challenge. "Anything you want to say to me, you can say right here."

CHAPTER TWO

J.D. LEANED AGAINST his car and rested one booted foot on the bumper. "You remind me of a horse I once owned," he said conversationally.

"A *what?*"

"A horse—an Appaloosa mare."

"Is that all you can talk about? Horses?" Deanna was surprised to find herself feeling slightly insulted.

J.D. ignored her. "She was a beautiful thing," he remembered. "Her lines were exquisite. She had the glossiest coat and the softest, prettiest eyes I ever saw. But she was also the stubbornest, most contrary mare I ever had the misfortune to ride. I can't tell you how many times I ended up on my backside in the dirt."

Deanna smiled at the image, then scowled as a thought struck her. "What happened to the poor creature? Did you force her to submit or sell her to the glue factory?"

J.D. shook his head. "Neither. I spent every spare minute trying to gain her trust and affection. Took me years. I'm still working at it."

"You didn't get rid of her?" Deanna was amazed.

"No. You see—" he gave her a slow, sensuous smile "—I like my females spirited."

As the full meaning of his words sunk in, Deanna blushed, and she was uncomfortably aware of the way his gaze was inspecting every inch of her.

She recovered quickly, however—or so she told herself. "Save your breath, Mr. Vaughn. I'm no teenager who's taken in by a few smooth though somewhat unoriginal lines. The old 'spirited filly' line is not only clichéd, it's also insulting." She gave him a look that let him know she would not be manipulated. "Your poor—and I emphasize *poor*—attempts at flattery won't get you Rustler."

"I'll settle for taking you to dinner."

Deanna's lips parted in amazement at his audacity. "You don't give up, do you?"

"Not even when the horse throws me," J.D. admitted with a grin. "I just climb right back on."

"I think all those falls have scrambled your brains. Read my lips, Mr. Vaughn. N-O. I'm going home."

"I don't think so. You see, I saw your mother take your keys out of your purse. And I locked the office door behind us. So unless you want to pound on it and beg your mother to let you in…" His eyes twinkled. "Tell me, is she as stubborn as you?"

Deanna was shocked by her mother's treachery. Helen had her own set of truck keys.

"I'm certain you wouldn't want to walk home, not after putting in such a hard day. Just how far away is your place?" he asked.

"A little over ten miles," Deanna replied in a tight voice. She glanced back to her office just as Helen put the Closed sign in the front window and lowered the blinds.

"It's awfully hot for a ten-mile hike. I'd say it's still in the nineties. But then, May's always hot in this part of Arizona." J.D. opened the passenger door of his car. "Go ahead and yell at your mother if it makes you feel better," he suggested. "I'll wait until you're ready to leave."

Deanna looked at him and saw the same expression on his face that Helen got when she insisted on cleaning the surgery. In fact, it was the same expression Deanna wore when her mind was made up. J. D. Vaughn wasn't going anywhere. He was as immovable as the Leighton women. Only Deanna would bet her last suture kit he had far more patience.

He'd be waiting by his fancy car until the ground swallowed them both up or Helen unlocked the office. And the former was about as likely to happen as the latter. Either way, the only thing that *would* happen was Deanna's embarrassing herself by making a scene.

She remembered how he'd helped with the unruly gelding and then pitched in to ease her workload. To refuse him would be churlish.

"That's not necessary." Deanna forced herself to speak graciously. "I'd be most grateful for a lift home."

"And dinner?"

Deanna swallowed hard. "You're very generous," she managed to say. "Thank you, Mr. Vaughn."

A glint of admiration came into his eyes. "You're welcome. And please, everyone calls me J.D."

Deanna couldn't bear to go *that* far, but J.D. didn't press the issue. He held open her door, then closed it and climbed in himself. "Where to, ma'am?"

"I wish you wouldn't call me that. It makes me feel like a senior citizen."

"Where to, Deanna?"

Deanna glared at his use of her first name. "You're very sure of yourself, aren't you?"

J.D. merely smiled in response.

"There aren't many places to eat," she said after a pause. "This isn't a big town. There's only a hamburger joint, a meat-and-potatoes diner and a Mexican food place."

"Does it serve authentic Mexican or just the watered-down American version?"

"They have great-tasting authentic dishes. But they're extremely spicy," Deanna warned.

"I'm game if you are. How do I get there?"

Deanna gave him directions and settled back for the ride to what was laughingly called downtown Cactus Gulch. The desert they drove through was spectacular, containing many different types of cacti, from the tiny, pale green prickly pears to the towering dark saguaros. But Deanna had made the trip so many times she ignored the familiar landscape. The man beside her held her interest, instead.

"Aren't you going to ask about my horse?" Deanna said when he made no move to initiate any conversation.

"I'd much rather talk about you."

Deanna mentally snorted. He was certainly full of shop-worn lines. Well, she wasn't falling for this one, either. "There's not much to tell."

"Of course there is. I know a little, but I'm sure there's more."

"And just what exactly do you know?"

J.D. shrugged, his hands steady on the steering wheel. "You're Deanna Rose Leighton, born in Arizona, age twenty-eight, only child of Carl and Helen Leighton. You went to the University of Arizona for both your pre-vet and veterinary studies. You're actively involved in animal rights, working locally with Veterinarians for Victims and Cactus Gulch's humane shelter."

"Actually several shelters," she corrected. Her animal-rights group was not just locally based; it had members statewide. Veterinarians for Victims provided free medical services for animals rescued from abusive owners. Tragically the humane society was forced to put down a lot of these animals because of a lack of funds for medical treatment, but VFV tried to save as many as possible and place them in caring environments.

"Equine medicine is your specialty," J.D. continued. "The local people are afraid that with your skills you'll soon be moving on to bigger and better things."

"You had me checked out!" A confused Deanna didn't know what to think about that.

"Actually I did the checking myself," he said calmly.

There was silence in the car. A tense silence on Deanna's part, not that J.D. seemed to notice. It wasn't until they'd arrived at Julio's, ordered and been served that Deanna found herself relaxing in his presence and their conversation resumed.

"What made you decide to become a vet?" J.D. asked, biting into his beef enchilada.

"My parents used to run a boarding stable. I was constantly around horses and always enjoyed working with them. Becoming a veterinarian just seemed liked a natural extension of my interest."

J.D. nodded in understanding. "That's pretty much the same way I became interested in quarter horses."

Deanna stiffened. "I don't think you can compare your situation to mine."

"Why not? Growing up on a cattle ranch in Colorado, I spent more time in the saddle than I did on the ground."

"Yes, but my interest in horses never extended to seeing them race around a track." She couldn't keep the bitterness from her voice.

J.D.'s fork froze below his mouth. He deliberately lowered it and rested it on the edge of his plate. "I get the distinct impression you don't approve of what I do for a living."

"You're right," Deanna said bluntly. "I don't approve."

J.D.'s eyes flashed at her put-down, but he spoke calmly. "Without racetracks, there would be no reason for breeders to work at improving bloodlines. Pari-mutuel wagering provides both the incentive and the capital necessary to maintain a purebred equine strain. If it weren't for racing, quarter horses and Thoroughbreds would only be found in history books.'' He studied her carefully. ''Is that what you want? Because that's what would happen without racetracks.''

''Let me rephrase. It's not the racetracks I disapprove of. It's you.''

''Me? Why?''

Deanna couldn't believe it. J.D. actually appeared astonished. ''Don't pretend you don't know!''

''Know what?''

''About my father.''

''I know your mother's a widow. It's been—what?—five years since he died.''

''Six,'' Deanna said. Six years, and she still remembered it as if it was yesterday. ''My father loved horses,'' she said in a controlled impassive voice. ''His stables were on the outskirts of Phoenix.''

J.D. remained silent, so she continued, ''But Dad loved racehorses even better. For years he'd go watch the races at Phoenix's Thoroughbred track—you know, Turf Paradise—and cheer on his favorites. Mom and I knew this, but he always swore he wasn't a gambler.''

Deanna took a deep breath. ''Unfortunately he never told us about the horse he secretly bought and stabled at *your* ranch.''

''*My* ranch?''

''Don't play games with me! Dad borrowed money and sold shares in the Thoroughbred to pay the exorbitant price you charged to train, board and race him. And when the horse hit a losing streak, the backers wanted out, leaving my father in debt up to his eyeballs.''

She managed a chilly smile. "Even worse, not only did he beg, borrow and steal to replace missing shareholders' money, he wrote bad checks to make bets on his own horse. But Dad's bets were as lousy as his horse's track record. The only good luck he had was a fatal heart attack—just before the police came to haul him away."

"I'm sorry." J.D. reached for her hand, but Deanna snatched it out of his reach. She refused to accept his phony sympathy.

"It was only then that we found out how deeply in debt Dad was. As if his death wasn't enough. We hadn't even known about the racehorse, let alone Dad's gambling and the bad checks, but we sure did by the time the police were through with us. We had to sell the stables and move north to Cactus Gulch."

"Money goes further in a small town?"

"That, and our old neighbors weren't—how shall I put this?—very supportive of our situation." Deanna remembered how their self-righteous neighbors had condemned Helen for not stopping her husband's gambling and nefarious business practices. "Mom found us a place to live and got a job working as a cashier in the local feed store. She hated it."

"It must have been very hard for the two of you."

"It was awful, especially for Mom. She blamed herself for a long while. She felt that if she'd known about everything, Dad would still be alive."

"That's not true, of course."

"No. She couldn't have prevented his heart attack any more than she could have prevented his gambling and stealing. According to his business partners, Dad thought that since he owned a boarding stable, he knew all there was to know about horses. He honestly believed he could make a go of it. He never realized that training and racing a

Thoroughbred wasn't the same as boarding pleasure mounts—which is exactly what Dad's dream horse finally ended up being sold as." Deanna's mouth twisted at the memory. "I doubt he would have appreciated the irony."

"Deanna, I'm so sorry. No one should have to go through that."

"The worst part was finding out about it after the fact." Deanna lifted her chin, not wanting his pity. "But we survived. Mom was tough. She refused to let me quit school and help out. She was adamant that I finish my pre-vet studies and go on to graduate school."

"You earned a scholastic scholarship to grad school, didn't you?"

"Yes, but those were hard times financially."

J.D. gazed at her threadbare clothes and well-worn boots. "And they still are?"

"We do just fine," Deanna said immediately. "My father was the grasping one when it came to money, not me or my mother."

There was no way she could tell him the whole painful story. That she was still paying her father's debts off. That the sale of their boarding stable hadn't been near enough to cover those old debts. That her father had even involved his wife in his illegal attempts to get money.

Deanna's heart went cold as she remembered the police coming to their house with a warrant for Helen's arrest. Apparently, besides writing bad checks all over Phoenix, Carl had forged his wife's signature on half of them. Helen herself hadn't been able to tell the difference between the forgery and her own handwriting. So Helen Leighton was held criminally liable. There had been no money for an expensive lawyer, and the court-appointed lawyer was too overworked to prepare a competent case. The twenty-two-year-old Deanna had been certain her mother would go to jail. In one final frantic appeal, she'd passionately begged the judge to be lenient.

"I've won a scholarship to veterinary school, Your Honor. I'm planning on starting my own practice. I'd have a good income! Please, place my mother on probation. If you do, I'll pay back all the money. I swear it!"

Deanna recalled those horrible moments in court, waiting for the judge to make his decision. Perhaps it was the fact that her mother had no prior record. Perhaps it was Deanna's plea. Maybe a combination of the two. Whatever the case, Deanna got her wish. She remembered her sweaty palms, her mother's white face, then her overwhelming relief when the judge agreed to probation if Deanna repaid the debt—relief that turned to horror when Helen fainted dead away.

Deanna stared out the window, instead of at the man across from her, totally missing his concern and compassion. Eventually she felt his eyes on her.

"I can see now why you don't want to deal with me," J.D. said quietly when she finally faced him again. "Your father's problems have soured you on racetracks, and anyone associated with them."

"You really are something else," Deanna spat out. "My father's problems soured me on *you*, Mr. Vaughn. *You* were the one who sold my father that pitiful Thoroughbred. *You* were the one who trained it for him and raced it for him. Tell me. Have you been unloading your useless horses on naive amateurs like my father for long, or is this something recent?"

"I'm not in the practice of *unloading* anything, Deanna. I did own a few Thoroughbreds back then," he admitted, "but they weren't doing as well as my quarter horses."

"So you sold them to unsuspecting people like my father," she accused him bitterly.

"No. I was just starting out and had decided that quarter horses were all I could handle at the time, at least until I became more established. I *did* sell the Thoroughbreds, but not as winning racers. I made full disclosures of their flaws to each would-be owner and priced each animal accordingly."

Deanna looked at him in complete disbelief.

"Deanna, I swear I didn't know about this!"

"Right." She refused to be taken in by that startled expression, the shock in his eyes. Obviously the man was a consummate actor. "And I'm the First Lady."

She started to rise and leave, but a strong hand caught her arm. His grip wasn't painful, but she recognized its strength. She wasn't going anywhere.

"I promise I'll look into this," he emphasized as he gently pulled her back down into her chair.

"And do what? Restore our family's good name? Pay all our debts? Bring my father back from the grave?" Deanna jerked her arm away from his grasp. "I know my father was wrong to jump blindly into a speculative venture. He was totally at fault when it came to swindling his shareholders. And yes, he had a gambling problem. But you're just as guilty, Mr. Vaughn. Because you saw an easy mark coming and took full advantage of him."

"I would *never* have sold a horse without acquainting the buyer with any possible problems!"

"Maybe that's true now," Deanna retorted. "But what about seven years ago, when you'd just bought your ranch? Money must have been tight, Mr. Vaughn. Just how far were you willing to go to get it?"

Her outburst had caused some of the other diners to stare at her, so Deanna abruptly lowered her voice. The last thing she and her mother needed was to be fodder for Cactus

Gulch's gossip mill. They'd had enough of that in their last home.

"And now you have the nerve to bring your innocent act around here and offer to buy my horse? What's the matter? Is your conscience bothering you? Because if it is, let's get one thing straight. You're far too late."

Deanna's torrent of words ended, and there was a long pause. Deanna was miserable. Why had she bothered to tell him all this? She was certain he knew, positive he was just pretending to be unaware of her family's situation. She watched J.D. and wondered what he could possibly say next. She was just about to try leaving again when he finally spoke.

"I'm truly sorry about your father."

"Sure you are. You probably don't even remember him."

"I've sold a lot of horses in the past seven years, Deanna," he said quietly.

"You have an awfully convenient memory. Not to mention conscience."

"I know you must be hurting, but you're wrong."

More lies, Deanna thought, but she'd had enough of arguing. She remained silent.

"I'll personally look into this matter. If you and your family suffered any injustice at my hands, I promise to make restitution."

"Don't waste your time, Mr. Vaughn," Deanna said dispiritedly. "Everything you did was perfectly legal. Not exactly ethical, but legal. My mother and I neither want nor need your charity."

J.D. hesitated before speaking. "I can see this conversation is painful for you. Perhaps we should save any further discussion until after I check my records."

"Perhaps we should simply end all discussion here," Deanna replied, some of her old spirit returning.

"No. There's still the matter of Rustler. At the risk of being obvious, has it ever occurred to you that selling your horse could solve all your money problems? The horse you own has an incredible pedigree. I'm willing to take a chance on your two-year-old."

"Rustler's not the only Thoroughbred stallion around. Why are you so interested in him?" she asked suspiciously.

"It's quite simple really. When I decided to make another attempt at Thoroughbred racing, I purchased a mare who'd caught my fancy. She didn't look like much, and she cost even less. But my instincts were right on the money. She's placed in every single race I've entered her in over the past two racing seasons. This particular mare is Rustler's dam."

"You own Rustler's mother?"

"Yes. I've made inquiries and found out that Rustler is her only offspring."

"So that's why you want Rustler. You think he's a sure thing."

"If he's half the racer his mother is, yes. By the time I'd discovered his existence, Rustler had been sold to his last owner."

"The one who abused him."

"Yes, only I didn't know that then. I tried more than once to buy Rustler, but without any luck. Still, I kept tabs on him. That's how I found out he'd been abused and placed with you by the humane society."

"And since your mare was making you so rich, you couldn't wait to rush right down here and put in your bid," Deanna said disdainfully. "So you could get richer."

"So I could start my own breeding program," J.D. corrected. "Think about it, Deanna. A stallion like yours could go for thousands of dollars, which is what I'm prepared to offer."

Deanna's head spun at the possibilities that occurred to her after J.D. named a specific figure. It would cover the debt and then some.

"I never considered Rustler as a way out of my financial worries," she said slowly, her wish to have nothing to do with J.D. warring with her practical side. The Leightons could certainly use the money. Her vet practice was a small one. Even though she made a good income, by the time the courts were through taking their share, there wasn't much left.

"Why not? You certainly don't need a potential champion for pleasure riding."

"Maybe, but I'm fond of him. I don't want to sell him. If his bloodline is as good as you say, I might just let him stand at stud."

"No. You couldn't charge much for a horse without any race experience. Rustler needs wins to justify the stud fees. He needs to be trained for the track. You're not equipped to do that."

"Which brings us right back to where we started. You see, Rustler's lame. So you can take your charitable offer and go home."

"Lame?"

"Lame. Oh, he's not as bad as when I rescued him. In fact, he's even healthy enough to be ridden hard. He'll take a good workout, but he still has a slight limp. He'll never race."

J.D. was silent for a few moments. Deanna carefully searched his face, but the crushing disappointment she expected to find was not there. Surprisingly, she was the disappointed one. J. D. Vaughn no longer had a reason to remain in town. Not that she wanted him to, of course.

"Maybe you'll find the horse you need in Phoenix," she forced herself to say.

J.D. studied her. "I'm not only looking for a Thorough-bred stallion. I'm also in the market for a good equine vet-erinarian."

"I already have a full-time practice. Even if I didn't, I'm not experienced in treating racehorse injuries," Deanna said promptly. Her involvement with J. D. Vaughn had gone far enough.

"Tendon and ligament problems and stress fractures are nothing you couldn't handle. Besides, I'm interested in putting you on retainer for general maintenance for the horses I acquire through the Adopt-a-Horse program."

"*You're* involved with that?"

She was familiar with the program, because she'd done charity work for it occassionally. The Bureau of Land Management oversaw placement of wild mustangs that had been captured to prevent overgrazing on government pre-serves. The Adopt-a-Horse program allowed individuals to adopt mustangs for a modest fee and proof of ability to provide adequate care.

"I don't work for them," J.D. explained. "But I do support them by adopting horses from them."

"What does a quarter-horse breeder do with unpapered mustangs?"

"Oh, this and that."

"Do you use them for cattle work?"

"No."

"Pleasure riding?"

"Not exactly."

Deanna's eyes narrowed. J.D. was being deliberately vague. "I'll be honest with you, Mr. Vaughn. I could use your business. But I don't like working in the dark. If you want me as your vet, I'd need to know exactly what those horses are being used for.''

Deanna could have bitten her tongue off the moment the words were out of her mouth. She had no intention of working for this unscrupulous rancher, yet here she was actually considering his proposal. She gave her head a shake, feeling as disoriented as a rider kicked by her mount.

"Strictly humane purposes, I assure you," J.D. replied with an engaging smile.

Deanna resisted his charm. "I'm sorry, but I'll still have to refuse. Considering my father's involvement with your ranch, I'm sure you'll understand my reason." Was it her imagination, or did J.D. finally look disappointed? Before she could change her mind, she quickly added, "I'm not in a position to be taking on new clients right now, anyway. I'm leaving town this Friday and have made arrangements for someone else to cover my practice."

"Why? When will you be back?"

It was Deanna's turn to be vague. "It's business, and I'm not certain."

J.D. started to say something, then stopped. He gave her a careful assessing look, leaving Deanna squirming in her chair and wondering what that shrewd mind of his was thinking. She waited tensely for his next words.

"If you're finished eating, I'm ready to take you home," was all he said.

Deanna sighed in relief. Thank goodness, now he'd be out of her life. She could get on with more important things—her work and the debt she had to pay off. So what if her life was dull, she told that nagging little voice that was plaguing her. The last thing she needed was the sort of excitement provided by J. D. Vaughn.

The drive home didn't take long. Both her practice and the ranch where she lived were close to Cactus Gulch.

"Take this turn," Deanna instructed. "Mom and I rent an apartment at this sheep ranch."

The apartment was the upper story of an equipment barn that had been converted into a spacious living area. Steps on the side of the barn led up to a little porch area with a swing.

"The owner lets me board my horse here free, in return for veterinary care. He pays for materials, but not my services. That's what's nice about small towns. The barter system still exists."

Deanna was aware she was babbling, something highly out of character. Besides, the last thing she should be doing was making small talk with the enemy.

J.D. listened, but said nothing. He waited politely until Deanna was finished speaking, then asked, "Have you ever ridden a green-broke horse?"

Deanna blinked at the sudden change in conversation. "It's bad enough I have to treat them," she replied honestly. "I try to stay away from riding them. I like my horses well-schooled."

He nodded and drove the car to the end of the long dirt drive, then parked it before continuing.

"Half-broke horses are funny things."

"Funny?"

"Hard to read. They blow hot and cold. One moment they cooperate, the next they want to throw you to kingdom come. It's up to the rider to decipher those mixed signals and decide whether or not the horse is a keeper. I'm usually pretty good at reading mixed signals." He shook his head in disbelief. "But you, Deanna Leighton, have me stumped."

He ignored her shocked gasp. *Was* she giving off mixed signals? He'd been involved in her father's downfall, for heaven's sake! So what if he was handsome, with a totally masculine air that had Deanna's nerves tingling? She was a doctor—she understood animal chemistry. She was also nobody's fool and wasn't about to be taken in by J.D.'s smooth-talking ways.

"The unexpected always captures my interest, Deanna, and you're the most unexpected thing that's happened to me in a long time. I think I'll stick around. Goodbye—for now."

Deanna stared at him, unable to answer. J.D. calmly returned her gaze, then started to go around to open her door. Deanna didn't wait. She opened it herself and hurried up to her apartment, feeling J. D. Vaughn's watchful eye on her every step of the way.

CHAPTER THREE

"YOU TURNED HIM down?" Helen Leighton's voice rose a full octave. "You turned one of this state's wealthiest quarter-horse breeders down?"

"I turned one of this state's most unscrupulous horse dealers down. We can't trust him, Mom. We both know that."

"We don't know that! Maybe he was telling the truth! Maybe he did tell your father that the horse he bought wasn't good racing material."

"And maybe I'll win the lottery," Deanna retorted. "Come on, Mom. He's as bad as any used-car salesman sticking an unsuspecting customer with a lemon. Dad's racehorse was no good, or J.D. wouldn't have sold him."

"That's a perfectly valid reason to sell a horse, especially for someone trying to make a name for himself in the racing business! Your father should have realized that."

"J. D. Vaughn should have *made* Dad realize it! Instead, he just took the money and ran."

"Deanna, darling, your father would simply have gone to another horse ranch."

"Where? Vaughn's place is only ten miles from our old boarding stable. Maybe if he'd told Dad he wasn't experienced enough to own a racehorse, maybe if he hadn't made it so convenient, Dad would have stopped his crazy schemes right there."

Helen shook her head in confusion. "Don't be so sure. Your father could have easily gone south to Phoenix to buy a horse, instead."

"That's a much longer drive. Dad would have had time to come to his senses. . . ."

Helen sighed. "Deanna, you're being irrational. Your father was obviously determined to buy a horse, but that's ancient history. I'm more concerned about the present. Mr. Vaughn wants you as his vet. I think you should accept his offer."

"You honestly want me to work for that man?" Deanna couldn't believe what she was hearing. "He deliberately sold my father a second-rate racehorse, and now he has the colossal nerve to ask me to sell him Rustler! He shows up seven years later as if nothing's happened!"

"Deanna, this is a small town. We don't have that many clients, and you know it. We need the money."

"Yes, but does a wealthy rancher like J. D. Vaughn really need another vet? He didn't bother offering me the job until he found out Rustler was lame. It smacks of charity to me. Or a guilty conscience. Either way, I'm not interested."

"You're being very foolish." Helen picked up a towel from the pile of unfolded laundry and shook it out with a vicious snap.

"I have my pride, Mom, and I draw the line at working in some trumped-up job." In spite of her mother's disapproval, Deanna refused to back down. "Besides, I had other reasons."

Helen dropped the towel and slapped her hands on her hips, the laundry forgotten. "Such as?"

"Well, you know I'll be gone for a week retracing the Arizona leg of the old Butterfield Stage route. Veterinarians for Victims is sponsoring the wagon drive, and my pledge paperwork is nowhere near ready. The last thing I need is to take on a new project."

Deanna was busy searching for donors for the VFV's annual charity fund-raiser. Vets for Victims organized the project, welcoming other animal-rights groups to participate, as well. All groups benefited, with Vets For Victims, the official host charity, receiving a modest percentage of the gross to benefit their own work.

Sponsors from all over the state had pledged money for each stagecoach, wagon or mounted rider that retraced the Arizona leg of the old Butterfield Trail. Although much of the first successful mail-and-passenger route across the United States had disappeared, parts of it still existed in Arizona's rugged wilderness.

As the trail was ripe with both history and scenic beauty, much excitement had been generated by this year's unique choice for a pledge drive. Not only would Deanna be riding Rustler along the famous old trail to raise money for her own favorite animal-rights group, she'd also be acting as veterinarian for any equine illness or injuries that came up.

"Mom, even if I reconsidered, you know I couldn't ask Silas to take on a new client like Mr. Vaughn," Deanna replied evenly, trying to end the argument. Silas Parker was the retired veterinarian who would take over Deanna's practice while she was gone. "I haven't even done an assessment of his animals. It wouldn't be ethical to have someone else do the initial workup."

"You could have told Mr. Vaughn you'd take him on as soon as you got back. For heaven's sake, Deanna, you'll only be gone a week!"

"There's another reason," Deanna said, continuing to fold laundry. "When I asked him what a racehorse breeder was doing acquiring unpapered horses from the Adopt-a-

Horse program, Mr. Vaughn was deliberately vague. For all I know, he could be selling them to the canneries!''

Deanna shivered at the thought. Horse meat made up the bulk of canned dog food. More than once the government had uncovered unscrupulous men who adopted the horses for nominal fees, then resold them to the canneries for a profit.

"He didn't seem like that kind of man to me. I'm certain Mr. Vaughn has money to spare without risking prosecution by abusing animals," Helen snapped. ''The least you could do is call the Adopt-a-Horse program yourself. You have friends there. Check him out!''

Deanna stared at her mother in frank surprise. "I didn't know you felt so strongly about all this."

"Of course I do! My own daughter has ransomed her life to pay my debts—"

"Dad's debts."

"And then she turns down a chance to buy back her freedom!''

"Don't be so dramatic." Deanna chuckled. "I'm not turning down anything...." Her amusement died as she saw the tears in her mother's eyes. "Mom, what's wrong?"

"Wrong? You ask me what's wrong? Your life is ruined because of me! You live in a tiny town that offers nothing for a woman your age. You work like a dog and give all your money to the courts. You don't even date!''

Deanna shrugged. "I've done my share. I'm not interested in casual dating anymore, Mom. I'd like a husband and children someday, but it's hardly fair to ask any man to take on all this. When the debts are paid off, I'll start socializing again, I promise.''

That was the wrong thing to say. Helen's face crumpled. "You'll be an old woman by then. You're twenty-eight, and you've been paying for so long already. Years from now, you'll still be paying! If I'd known this would happen, I'd have gone to jail, instead!''

Horrified, Deanna dropped the shirt she'd been folding. "Don't say that! Don't you *ever* say that!''

"I mean every word,'' Helen sobbed. "First your father failed you, then I did. We've both ruined your life.''

Deanna threw her arms around her mother and held her tight. She patted Helen's shoulder, ignoring the tears that came to her own eyes.

"Mom, please don't. I'll call up the people at Adopt-a-Horse first thing tomorrow, okay? If J. D. Vaughn is legitimate, I'll seriously consider taking him on as a client,'' Deanna promised.

Helen continued to cry, her face buried in her hands. Only the gray-streaked top of her head was visible. Deanna silently cursed J. D. Vaughn for yet another offense—hurting the one person in the world who deserved it the least.

"Mom, if you stop, I'll call them right now,'' Deanna said frantically. "Right this minute. Is it a deal?''

With an effort, Helen strived for control. She sniffed and nodded. Deanna hurried to bring her a tissue, then retrieved the phone book.

"I'm calling,'' she announced, her eyes darting back and forth between the phone buttons and her mother. "Do you want to listen in?''

Helen dabbed at her cheeks, shaking her head.

"It's ringing, Mom. I—Hello, this is Dr. Deanna Leighton. May I speak to Kathy Tomlinson in processing, please? Thank you.''

Deanna held her hand over the mouthpiece. "The switchboard is putting me through. You remember Kathy, right? She'll be coming along on the Butterfield route, too.''

Helen nodded in answer.

"Kathy? Hello, it's Deanna Leighton."

"Deanna, hi! Are we on for the weekend? I'm still taking your gear in my stagecoach, right?"

"Yes, there's been no change. As far as I know, everything's all set. I'm not calling about the fund-raiser, Kathy. I need a reference from the Adopt-a-Horse program for a rancher. His name's J. D. Vaughn."

"Oh, you mean Dallas Vaughn, the ex-rodeo star? What a great guy. And he isn't hard on my eyes, either."

Deanna rolled her eyes as Kathy, a happily married woman with a fifteen-year-old son, sighed like a swooning teenager.

"I don't need to know what he looks like, Kathy. I've seen him. And his being an ex-rodeo star doesn't impress me in the least. In fact, quite the opposite."

Veterinarians for Victims had been called to more than one rodeo to investigate claims of abused livestock. Deanna herself couldn't understand why rodeos were still so popular. She personally felt they were as outdated as bullfights.

"I need to know what J.D. does with all those horses he adopts," Deanna asked. "Why would a quarter-horse breeder bother with unpapered stock?"

"You don't know?"

"No, I don't," Deanna said patiently. "That's why I'm calling. Why's he involved with Adopt-a-Horse?"

"Well, you know J.D.'s from a ranching family in Colorado."

Deanna reined in her impatience and prepared to sit through a lengthy conversation. Kathy wasn't exactly known for getting right to the point.

"A big family, too, come to think of it. If I'm not mistaken, he's the second youngest of six children."

"Six?"

"Yes. Five boys and one girl named Sierra. She lives in southern Arizona, by the way. As a matter of fact, that's how Dallas—J.D.—ended up settling in Arizona permanently. He and his sister are quite close. Her husband is a native Arizonan, and after Sierra married, J.D. decided to go to college in Phoenix. Eventually he stayed."

"Kathy, this is all very... fascinating, but I'm more interested in his involvement with mustangs."

"But he'd be perfect for you!" Kathy insisted. "I've peeked at his files and I can give you the latest scoop!"

"Forget the scoop. You know I don't like anyone trying to fix me up."

"I know, I know, but don't you even want to hear if he's married or not?"

Deanna realized she was curious. "I just assumed he was. He's attractive enough for most women, I suppose."

"More than most," Kathy chided. "But believe it or not, he's not married."

"Really?" Deanna couldn't keep the enthusiasm out of her voice. Much to her dismay, Kathy immediately picked up on it.

"Interested, Deanna?"

"No," Deanna replied stiffly. Really, her friend's matchmaking efforts were so blatant! Subtlety was not Kathy's strong point. "Besides, you were the one who brought his marital status up, not me. I told you, I only want to know what J.D.'s connection to Adopt-a-Horse is."

Deanna decided she hadn't sounded very convincing when she heard Kathy's next words.

"J.D. had a serious girlfriend he met while on the rodeo circuit, but they broke up a while ago. No hard feelings, I understand. He told me all about it."

"I bet you dragged it out of him," Deanna guessed, embarrassed by her friend's outright nosiness.

Kathy didn't bother to deny it. "He's dated quite a few women since then, but they don't last long."

Deanna refused to voice her next thought. *I wonder why...* It didn't matter, though, Kathy was more than happy to provide the answer.

"He doesn't like flashy women, and there seems to be a lot of them in the racing business."

Wild horses couldn't have prevented Deanna from asking, "What kind of women *does* he like?"

"Oh, down-to-earth types. Wholesome and honest. You know, like yourself. Too bad you aren't interested," Kathy said slyly. "J.D. likes his women smart."

Deanna felt her heart give a traitorous skip. To make amends, she forced herself to say, "I don't want to date the man. I just want to know what he does with the horses he adopts."

Kathy laughed. "If I didn't respect you so much, Dr. Leighton, I'd call you an out-and-out liar."

"Kathy..." Deanna said warningly.

"All right, all right. Your J.D.—"

"He's not *mine*."

Kathy ignored the interruption. "J. D. Vaughn adopts horses for a friend of his."

"Can't this friend adopt them himself?"

"He could, but Matt Caldwell's not a horseman. He knows how to ride, but not how to pick good horseflesh."

Deanna felt her frustration rise. Helen was hanging on to every word of Deanna's side of the conversation, and Kathy was proving to be quite long-winded.

"Then what *is* he?"

"Matt's a recreational therapist. He works with mentally and physically challenged youngsters on his dude ranch in Colorado. Whenever Matt needs horses, he calls J.D. They were best friends in high school," Kathy explained. "Anyway, J.D. picks out the most even-tempered animals he can find, pays the adoption fees, then breaks and trains them for Matt. And get this, Deanna, J.D. does it free of charge."

"Free of charge?" Deanna echoed in amazement. She knew how much money a good horse trainer could command. It was no small piece of change, especially if the horses had to be trained for riders with special needs.

"That's right. J.D. won't take a cent from Matt. Says he won't earn money off children. Insists he's glad to do it and rips up every check Matt sends. Matt refuses to stop sending them, and J.D. refuses to stop destroying them. The two men have been fighting over this for years, but each is as stubborn as the other. That's probably why they've remained friends for so long. They're a lot alike."

"Good Lord!" Deanna said with respect and grudging admiration.

Helen looked up at Deanna's exclamation, but Deanna only held one finger in the air and motioned Helen to wait. Deanna was having a hard time assimilating the news. It didn't fit her preconceptions about J.D. It appeared he had a few redeeming features, after all.

"J.D. underwrites his training and boarding costs with his quarter-horse business," Kathy continued. "Can you believe it?"

Deanna's head spun. If Kathy's information was true and if he hadn't been responsible for her father's downfall, she'd be very tempted to follow up on the obvious interest J.D. had shown in her.

It almost made her wish he *hadn't* been responsible. . . .

"Anyway, the Adopt-a-Horse program gives J.D. all the horses he wants. They get exceptional care and good homes under both his hands and Matt's. J.D. gets our highest recommendation, Deanna. If it was up to me, I'd nominate the man for sainthood—or at least, try to make him some single woman's husband. He's generous, compassionate, intelligent and good-looking to boot. What more could you want from a man?''

Deanna didn't know what to say to that. After a moment, Kathy asked, ''Do you have any other questions?''

''No, I think that about covers it.'' And then some, she thought. But her annoyance at Kathy's tendency to gossip had long vanished.

''I can put a recommendation in writing for you, if you want.''

''That won't be necessary.'' Deanna slowly exhaled. ''Thanks, Kathy.''

''Anytime. I'll see you this weekend. 'Bye, Deanna.''

''Goodbye.'' Deanna hung up the phone, her eyes thoughtful. It wasn't until Helen called her name twice that Deanna met her mother's gaze.

''Well?'' Helen asked. ''What's the verdict?''

''I'll contact Mr. Vaughn first thing in the morning and make arrangements to go out to his ranch. I'm not promising anything, but I will look into seeing if he really has enough work to justify putting me on retainer.''

''So he checks out?''

''Yes. In fact,'' Deanna said dryly, ''he seems almost too good to be true. I can't believe our luck.''

Helen smiled and began folding the laundry again. ''It's about time a little luck came our way.''

Deanna couldn't bring herself to spoil her mother's cheerful mood. The whole situation kept nagging at her. In her experience, whenever something seemed too good to be true, it usually meant trouble.

And trouble was something that the Leightons could do without, no matter how charming the package it arrived in.

DEANNA TOOK a deep breath and drove her truck up to the security gates of the Rocking J. She'd stalled long enough, driving the fifty miles to the ranch at far less than the posted speed limit. She might as well get this over with. Helen's emotional outburst yesterday had Deanna worried. Carl Leighton had been dead for six years. It wasn't like Helen to suddenly question their lives. Deanna had long ago accepted her father's failings and the effect they'd had. Until yesterday, she'd thought Helen had, too. Trust the enemy to come into town and confuse things.

The guard at the security gate cleared her, and Deanna stepped on the accelerator and drove down the long, paved drive. Acres of paddocks surrounded her, while the smell of horses and freshly cut alfalfa filled the air. The guard had told her simply to follow the road to the end. The main offices were there.

Ah, there was a sign neatly indicating the offices. A guard met her as she parked her truck. She was escorted out to one of the yearling pastures, pointed toward the barn she was assured held J.D., then left alone.

After a quick admiring look at the yearlings in the pasture, Deanna headed into the barn.

"Good morning." J.D. noticed her immediately. "I see you're an early riser, too." There was a cheerful glint in his eyes, and he gave her a broad smile. "Come on in," he invited, still holding a foal firmly by its lead.

Deanna hesitated, staring at his bare chest and the colt at his side. "Am I interrupting? I didn't mean to disturb you, but I need to get back to my practice before it opens...." Her voice drifted off as she noticed his washboard stomach. Kathy's comment—"He isn't hard on the eyes"— suddenly came to mind. Deanna swallowed and fought against a sudden rush of physical attraction. "Maybe I should go wait in your office."

"Nonsense. Your timing couldn't be better. This little guy's hurt himself playing with some of the bigger yearlings. I can't tell if he needs stitches or not. I could use an expert's opinion."

Only then did Deanna notice the blood on the colt's left flank and on J.D.'s hands.

She looked out toward the faraway parking lot. "I'll have to get my bag. It's in the truck."

"That won't be necessary. I have a kit right here."

She hurried over to the kit resting on a hay bale behind them, making certain to keep her eyes away from his torso. *Mom's right,* Deanna thought wryly. *I have been out of circulation for too long if a bare chest can affect me like this. Next I'll be getting sweaty palms like a schoolgirl on prom night.* Somehow she managed to present a professional air. "I'll be glad to help, Mr. Vaughn."

"Won't you call me J.D.?" he asked.

"If you wish, J.D." Surprisingly the initials rolled easily off her tongue. "This colt's not very big. If you can hold him still, that'd be great. I can do without a twitch for at least the initial exam."

J.D. patted the brown neck. "He's pretty calm. I'll keep him quiet."

Deanna nodded. She removed the materials she needed, then gently approached the colt to clean the wound. "Some topical antibiotic should fix him up," she announced after a couple of minutes.

"He won't need any stitches?"

"No. The cut's long, but not deep. It looks like he was caught by an unshod hoof. There'll probably be some bruising, but that can't be helped. Just keep it clean and apply the ointment three times a day until it's gone. He should be fine." Deanna smiled at the colt and ventured a light pat on his nose. "I'd keep him away from the others until the wound scabs over."

"Will do. Thanks, Deanna." Deanna watched J.D. turn to take the colt back to his stall, then gasped. J.D.'s back was covered with ugly scars.

"Not very pretty, are they?" he remarked casually. He didn't break stride, although he did glance at her over his shoulder.

"Good Lord, what happened?" Deanna continued to stare at the puckered ridges of flesh.

"Those are compliments of a hungry Colorado grizzly I met in my youth. He was after the family cattle, and I got in the way."

He released the colt's lead and closed the stall door. "My sister shot and killed the bear, but not before the bear killed my horse and clawed my back. I was thirteen at the time."

"Only thirteen?"

J.D. shrugged. "Ranch life is no picnic."

He rinsed the colt's blood off his hands in the barn's sink, then dried off. He neatly hung his used towel above the sink, and that action alone told Deanna he was a man used to taking care of himself. Most people using a barn sink would have just tossed the towel on the floor. J.D. reached for his shirt resting atop the same hay bale where she'd found the medical kit. It was another silk shirt, Deanna noticed.

"I learned my lesson, though," he said. "Sierra was only twelve, but she was a dead shot—unlike me. I spent a lot more hours practicing with my rifle when I got out of the hospital."

"And now?" Deanna asked as he shook out strands of alfalfa clinging to the shirt.

"Now I'm a dead shot, too. Not that I run into many grizzlies at the racetrack." He grinned. "Still, you never know."

"I guess." And then, because the thought of J.D.—of anyone, she told herself—going through such an ordeal upset her more than she cared to admit, Deanna changed the subject. "Aren't those shirts a little dressy for everyday wear?" she asked curiously.

"You mean impractical," he corrected without rancor as he slid his arms into the sleeves. "And yes, they are. But I grew up on a cattle ranch. All I wore were flannel work shirts in the winter and cotton work shirts in the summer. When I left home, I swore I'd never wear another. And I haven't."

"You hated the shirts that much?"

"No, I hated working cattle that much. Western shirts remind me of cattle. Ornery witless beasts. I always preferred horses."

Deanna gazed with envy at the rich material as he rolled up first the left, then the right cuff. "Surely you wear something else when you train your horses?"

"Nope. Ever since I left the rodeos, it's been silk or nothing. My one vanity."

Deanna blinked at his honesty. "You must go through a lot of shirts."

"I've worked hard for the privilege," he said quietly.

Deanna had no reply. She watched as he reached for his watch, which he'd also taken off earlier. The band was a huge hunk of turquoise-studded silver that matched his belt buckle.

Deanna's face lighted up in admiration for the craftsmanship. "What a beautiful piece of work!"

"Thank you. My sister had an Indian friend of hers make up a three-piece set for me for Christmas a few years ago. There's a matching bola-string tie to go with it, but I was never one for ties except at weddings and Sunday services," he admitted. "You like turquoise?"

"I love it. It's my birthstone—I was born in December."

J.D. nodded. "Then you probably have a few pieces yourself."

"No, I don't." Except for the cheap watch she wore, Deanna had no jewelry at all. Anything else of value that she and her mother had owned, including her turquoise, had been pawned long ago and put toward the debt. "I'd be afraid to wear fine jewelry in my line of work." Of course she couldn't tell him the real state of affairs—though for some reason, Deanna felt he would understand if she did.

J.D.'s eyes narrowed, but he accepted her explanation without comment. He put away the medical kit and checked on the colt one last time. Next he walked her outside the barn and over to the yearling pasture. Beyond that, far off in the distance, Deanna could see the racetrack where the quarter horses were being worked.

She paused for a moment to watch their running sprints, their great speed impressive even at this distance. Then she turned to watch the yearlings. The playful antics of the young horses appealed to her more than the racing workouts.

J.D. waited until he had her attention again before asking, "Now, shall we talk business?"

"About that job you offered me," Deanna said slowly. "If you're still interested in putting me on retainer as a vet for your horses . . ."

Deanna saw J.D.'s eyes glitter with a strange emotion. Satisfaction? No, *triumph.*

"I am," he said.

"Then I might be your man."

He gave her a slow dangerous look that had Deanna's hormones reacting.

"Figuratively speaking, of course," she added before she made a fool of herself by blushing. Heavens, she was too old for this silliness. "I'm not making any commitment yet. I'd like to find out exactly what the job entails before I decide."

"There's no time like the present. I've freed up my morning to show you around." He gestured toward the expansive paddocks and their accompanying barns, then hooked one foot on the fence's lowest rail. "We can take as long as you like."

"Unfortunately I can't be long, J.D. I have to get back to work."

"All right, I'll show you as much as I can before you have to leave. If we run out of time, we could get together in, say, a week and a half? That should give you plenty of time to recover from your charity drive."

"I never told you about that! How did you find out?"

He shrugged.

"Don't give me that 'aw, shucks' look," she said irritably. "No one in town knows I'm going away except my replacement and my—" Deanna stopped abruptly as a most disturbing suspicion entered her mind.

Mother, you didn't! You wouldn't!

But her mother had, Deanna realized without a doubt. And Lord knew what else the normally closemouthed Helen Leighton had revealed. The last thing Deanna wanted was this man knowing everything about her family's misfortune. Her mother's criminal conviction was no one's business. The last time Helen had made the mistake of sharing their family's problems, it had been disastrous. She'd become a social outcast overnight, and they'd been forced to move.

"Is something wrong?" J.D. asked, but Deanna wasn't fooled by him for a minute.

"Tell me," she said in her coldest voice. "Just what else has my mother told you?"

CHAPTER FOUR

Deanna watched impatiently as J.D. removed his foot from the railing and slowly pivoted to face her. She knew a delaying tactic when she saw one.

"Well?" she demanded. "Are you going to answer my question?"

"There's not much to say," he replied. "Your mother called and told me to expect you this morning. That's about it."

J.D.'s expression was carefully blank. Damn his poker face! Well, it didn't matter. Deanna would question Helen later.

"Your mother's quite a lady. Thinks the world of you. I hope you don't intend to grill her about something so inconsequential."

Deanna almost jumped out of her skin. Was he a mind reader? "I wouldn't do that."

"I'm glad. I'd hate to think you were the kind of daughter who didn't let her mother live her own life," J.D. said. "After all, she's a grown woman."

"I'm used to looking after her. That's what a daughter's supposed to do."

"Only if your mother wants it. Or needs it."

"Of course she needs it! If you only knew—" Deanna sputtered and stopped.

"Only knew what?"

About her mother's debts? About the probation officer Helen reported to every month? About the threat of jail hanging over her head? It was time to find out exactly how much J. D. Vaughn did know.

"You said you were going to check out my father's business dealings with your ranch. Have you?"

"Yes."

Deanna forced herself to speak calmly. "And what did you find out?"

"Your father did buy a Thoroughbred from me back when I was just starting up the Rocking J. My quarter-horse racers were bringing in the money, but my Thoroughbreds were a risky proposition. I didn't have the financial security back then that I do now, so I sold them."

"And my father was only too happy to take one of them off your hands." Deanna sighed. What an unfortunate combination—Carl Leighton, desperate to buy a Thoroughbred racehorse, and J. D. Vaughn, desperate to unload one.

"The horses I sold were good stock that couldn't quite cut it on the track. They were healthy, they were hearty, but they weren't Kentucky Derby winners. Nor would they ever be. I did emphasize that, Deanna."

He sounded sincere, but somehow Deanna couldn't quite bring herself to believe him, not even when his gaze locked with hers. There was an awkward pause.

Finally she said, "It was a long time ago. I guess it doesn't matter either way."

"It matters to me, Deanna. And I think it matters to you, too."

He was right, of course. Still, Deanna refused to admit it.

"What else did you find out?" She had to ask. If J.D. knew about her mother's trial as Carl Leighton's coconspirator, Deanna would know for certain that his offer of a job was charity, after all.

"Why? What else is there?" he said.

"I, um—" she thought fast under his sharp scrutiny "—was wondering if perhaps my father left any outstanding debts? You know, boarding and training costs."

"Oh, that." The curiosity on his face faded. "No, everything was paid in full. After your father's death, his shareholders had me sell the horse for them."

"I knew that."

"Well, the proceeds from that sale covered everything owed to me," J.D. told her.

Deanna breathed a sigh of relief, but it was for more than just the settled account. She was especially relieved that J. D. Vaughn hadn't heard the whole story. Fortunately the newspapers hadn't bothered to cover her mother's trial. Writing bad checks and getting probation for it was hardly front-page news. If J. D. Vaughn hadn't discovered the truth, then she doubted anyone in Cactus Gulch had, either.

"Deanna, about that vet job..." J.D.'s voice broke into her thoughts. "I really do need someone. I'm getting a lot more horses in, and my present vet already has a busy practice. He's having a hard time meeting my needs."

"I'm sorry," Deanna replied, "but I can't give you a decision right now." She still didn't believe J.D. was completely blameless when it came to her father's misfortune. She'd have to think long and hard about accepting a position with him.

"Because of your father." It was a statement, not a question. Deanna was glad he wasn't pretending he didn't understand.

"Exactly. The two of you met because of a Thoroughbred, and now the two of us meet because of Rustler, another Thoroughbred. There's no denying..." She paused. The unpleasantness? The bad memories? The strain on Helen, not to mention herself? "The irony of it all," she finished.

"No, I imagine this isn't easy for you. But I really do need another vet."

"I'll think it over and give you my final decision as soon as I get back from my charity ride. Will that be soon enough?"

"It'll do."

"Well..." Deanna reached into her pocket for her truck keys and gave them a meaningful jingle. "I do have to get to work. I'd best be going." She stepped away from the paddock railing and back onto the path that led to the parking lot. "I'll be in touch."

"Don't take too long, Deanna, or I'll be contacting you myself."

"I don't doubt it for a moment," Deanna replied dryly. But deep inside, she couldn't deny the spark of pleasure she felt at his words. She also couldn't help being unsettled by it, or the way the memory of his scarred back and broad shoulders kept intruding into her thoughts. That probably accounted for her waspishness when she got back to work. She was even short with Helen.

"Mother, you promised you'd reorder that DHLP vaccine for me days ago!" Deanna complained. "I only have four vials left. What am I supposed to tell my patients when I run out?"

Helen paused. They were between cases, and Helen had just entered the small examining room with the next chart.

"The distributor was late, but promised our shipment would be in tomorrow. I told you yesterday, Deanna. Don't you remember?"

"No, I don't. Are you sure you mentioned it?"

Helen frowned. "I thought I did ... but I could be mistaken."

"Maybe if you concentrated on talking to me instead of J. D. Vaughn, I'd be better informed."

"Talking to ... ? Oh, so that's what this is all about— Your bad temper and my being 'Mother' instead of 'Mom.'"

Deanna didn't deny it. "It was bad enough when you lifted my keys out of my purse so I had to eat with the man. I kept quiet about it, not that I approved of your little stunt. But when you start filling in a perfect stranger about my private life, I have to draw the line!"

"I merely called and told him to expect you," Helen said in her most dignified manner. "That's hardly telling him your most intimate secrets. Not that you have any, thanks to the dull life you lead. I'll bet nuns in a convent have more fun."

Deanna gasped, but quickly recovered. "The kind of life I lead is my choice. I don't need you, or Kathy, or anyone else, for that matter, trying to liven it up by playing matchmaker. Especially considering J.D.'s history with Dad—or have you forgotten?"

"No, I haven't forgotten, Deanna. As if you'd ever let me." There was censure in Helen's voice. "J.D. seemed to like you, and he's a prospective customer for your services. I was just trying to help."

"Well, don't. Let me run my business, *and* my personal life, my own way. I'm quite capable."

"As you wish. I didn't mean to upset you. Now if you don't mind, I'll call in the next patient before checking with the distributors again."

"Mom, don't be mad," Deanna pleaded, already sorry she'd been so harsh. "I just want ..."

But it was too late. Helen was gone. The tension between them lasted for the rest of the day and, in fact, for the rest of the week.

Helen was still cool and standoffish the day Deanna was to leave for the charity ride. She was packed and waiting for Kathy to pick her up when a very quiet Helen came outside to see her off.

"You know how to contact me in case of an emergency?" Deanna asked. The wagon train would be carrying a radio, and she could be reached that way.

"Yes."

"And you'll make certain Silas knows where everything is?" Deanna knew her substitute vet was sometimes a bit absentminded.

"Yes."

"You'll be all right without me?"

"Yes."

Deanna mentally sighed at the monosyllable answers. Helen was being difficult, courtesy one J. D. Vaughn. Well, Deanna would be getting away from him for a whole week. If she was lucky, he'd have found a new vet for his ranch by the time she returned. Deanna would be off the hook, and her mother would be back to her normal cheerful self.

Beside her, Rustler tugged against his bridle, his glossy chestnut coat glistening in the desert sunshine. Deanna automatically checked the tightness of the stallion's lead on the hitching post.

"Well, here's my ride." She gestured toward Kathy's truck, which had just turned down their dusty drive.

Helen said nothing.

Deanna busied herself with loading Rustler into the trailer. The scent of other horses lingering in the trailer made him somewhat skittish, but Deanna soon had him calmed down and secured. She then loaded her saddle and packs into the storage space up front.

Turning to Helen, she said awkwardly, "I guess I'd better be going. Do I get a hug goodbye?"

For a moment Deanna thought she'd refuse, but then her mother's arms were tightly around her.

"You take care of yourself, Deanna," Helen whispered.

"You, too, Mom. I'm sorry I was so short-tempered. I didn't mean it."

"I know. I didn't, either. Deanna—you *do* know I love you?"

Deanna pulled away in surprise. "Of course I do. Mom, it was only a little tiff. You know how I get sometimes."

Helen shook her head. "It was more than that." Suddenly tears came to her eyes. "No matter what happens, I want you to promise me that you'll remember."

"Remember what?"

"That I love you."

"Mom . . ." Deanna said, confused and worried by Helen's odd mood.

"Promise me."

"I promise, but . . . are you all right?"

Helen nodded vigorously and patted Deanna's shoulder. "You'd better get going now. You don't want to keep Kathy waiting. Have a good trip."

"I will." Deanna gave her mother another hug and kissed her on the cheek. "Now don't you work too hard. I hired a local man to help clean the kennels and surgery, so you let him do most of the heavy stuff, okay?"

"Okay. And you be careful riding Rustler."

"I will."

"Watch him around the mares. He *is* a stallion, you know."

Deanna laughed, glad to see some of Helen's animation return. "I know, Mom." She climbed into the oversize cab of the truck, where Kathy and her fifteen-year old son, Shawn, were waiting. "I'll call you if I can. Goodbye!"

Helen lifted her hand in farewell, but there was no farewell smile on her face. Deanna felt a sudden sense of foreboding, but Kathy was already driving away. There was nothing Deanna could do but say a prayer that Helen would be fine without her.

Kathy gave Deanna a curious look. "Everything okay?"

"I hope so, but I don't know. My mother hasn't been herself lately."

Kathy glanced in the rearview mirror. "She looks tired. Maybe she needs some time off. The two of you work awfully hard."

Deanna shook her head. "Maybe." She was worried, yet unable to do anything about it.

"Hey, snap out of it," Kathy urged. "Helen's a grown woman. She'll be all right."

Deanna started in surprise. "You know, you're the second person who's said that to me lately."

"There you go. Helen has a sensible head on her shoulders. And face it, Deanna, you two probably need a break from each other. It can't be easy for a mother and daughter to live *and* work together."

"I suppose." Deanna still didn't feel reassured, but she let Kathy's jovial personality put her into a better frame of mind.

Kathy Tomlinson was closer to Helen's age than Deanna's, but she acted more like her fifteen-year-old son than a respectable matron. She was fiercely loyal, crazy about horses and had a happy-go-lucky attitude that endeared her to everyone. Kathy's stockbroker husband was a stern but loving man who tended to indulge Kathy's free spirit.

Shawn was a quiet young boy who—unlike most teenagers—adored his unconventional mother and wasn't afraid to show it.

Deanna was comfortable in their company and had eagerly accepted Kathy's offer to carry Deanna's provisions in the Concord stagecoach Adopt-a-Horse provided.

"It's a long drive to the Arizona-New Mexico border," Kathy said with a sigh after a while.

"But that's where the old Butterfield Trail began in southern Arizona," Deanna reminded her. "At Stein's Peak Station on the border."

"At least once I'm there I'll be driving the stage. Adopt-a-Horse sent the coach and team ahead. I hate driving the truck," Kathy complained, "especially when I have to tow the horse trailer."

"I'll spell you if you want," Deanna offered. She reached into her jeans for a barrette and clipped her long black curls back from her face. "We can switch next time we stop for gas."

"You don't mind?"

"Not a bit. After all, you're doing me a favor by hauling Rustler. I don't have a horse trailer of my own."

"Thanks, I'll take you up on it." Kathy grinned. "I can't wait until Shawn gets his license this fall. I'm never going to drive this truck again—to heck with the higher insurance rates. Whatever it costs to cover Shawn, I'm paying. He can chauffeur me around. I know he'll be a good driver."

Shawn smugly preened in the back seat, and Deanna smothered a laugh. "I wonder if many other mothers of driving-age teenagers would share your sentiments."

Kathy threw Deanna an amused glance, then addressed her son. "Who cares? You only live life once, right, sweetheart?"

Deanna assumed that Shawn nodded, or that Kathy was used to his silence, as no answer was forthcoming. She waited a few seconds longer, but when Shawn had nothing to add, Deanna felt it was safe to change the subject.

"So did you get any other sponsors for the program?" she asked. Kathy was the official representative of Adopt-a-Horse, and all the monies pledged to her would benefit them.

"Oh, a few more high rollers from my husband's office. Shawn got a nice donation from one of his teachers at school, and then he had the kids in his class hit up their parents. He did an excellent job." Kathy beamed with maternal pride, and Deanna congratulated him.

"How large was your total pledge?" she asked.

Kathy named the figure, then shoved aside Deanna's praises. "Yes, it's good, but it's nowhere near as high as your total pledge. You offered your professional services to VFV but you've canvased sponsors for Adopt-a-Dog, right?"

"Yes."

The greyhound-racing industry had recently been criticized for its treatment of greyhounds. Young, healthy dogs that weren't winners were coldheartedly destroyed or simply abandoned by their owners.

Deanna was incensed by the waste and cruelty, both as a veterinarian and as an animal lover, so she'd made the greyhounds' plight her special concern for this drive. The pledges she received would be used by Adopt-a-Dog to place retired greyhounds in private homes. The charity was run along the same lines as the Adopt-a-Horse program.

Unfortunately Deanna's sponsors were few. So, how could her pledges surpass those made to Adopt-a-Horse?

"Kathy, you know I didn't get many sponsors. This is horse country. Even though Tucson has greyhound tracks, everyone wants to back Adopt-a-Horse. Adopt-a-Dog hasn't had nearly the publicity or support."

"A shame."

"I agree. I was lucky to get the money I did, but my tally isn't close to yours."

"But it is," Kathy insisted. "It's actually larger than mine."

Even the normally silent Shawn roused himself to say, "That's right, Dr. Leighton. Mom saw the figures."

Deanna tilted her head, puzzled. "Just how much *is* pledged toward my charity?"

"According to the latest printouts..." Kathy named an outrageous figure that made Deanna's jaw drop in amazement.

"That can't be right! There must be some mistake. I'll have to talk to the chairman and get it corrected. It's probably a computer error—some secretary putting the decimal point in the wrong place or something."

"Oh." Kathy's face fell. "And Shawn and I were so happy for those poor little dogs." Her face brightened almost at once. "Well, we'll just have to adopt one ourselves. How about it, Shawn? We only have horses at home. Shall we get ourselves a greyhound to help out the cause?"

"Let's get two," Shawn said. "One for me, and one for you and Dad. But I'll take care of both of them," he added generously.

"It's a deal, son."

For some time, Deanna listened as mother and son happily argued over what to name the proposed additions to the family. The conversation was cheerful, but it made Deanna sad. When would she have a husband and family? Would the day ever come when she could stop envying her friend?

Unbidden, the image of J. D. Vaughn popped into her mind. He was good with both people and animals, judging by the way he'd helped out at her clinic. She suspected he'd be just as good with children. But it didn't matter, even if she was madly in love with him, which she wasn't. There was no room for a man in her life—not J. D. Vaughn, not anyone.

Anyway, he wasn't her type. If she wasn't a bit lonely, she wouldn't even be thinking about him. Maybe she'd adopt a greyhound herself. Money was tight at home, but surely a little greyhound wouldn't cost much to feed. And his vet care would certainly come cheap.

That's what I need, Deanna decided. *A faithful pooch to keep me company.*

The rest of the drive went smoothly. As promised, Deanna took over the driving and tried to concentrate on the road, instead of J. D. Vaughn. It wasn't easy, especially since after a while both Kathy and Shawn dozed off and there was no conversation to distract her.

It was late afternoon when they finally reached the starting point for the charity drive.

"Here we are," Deanna said, rousing her sleeping companions. "Everyone wake up."

Kathy blinked, then straightened in her seat. "What time is it?"

"After four. I couldn't take the hills very fast with the horse trailer. Where do you want me to park the truck?"

"Wherever you can find a spot. We'll have to sign in before we unload. Why don't I stay here while you do that?" Kathy suggested.

"Are you sure? I have to talk to the chairman about that pledge mistake for Adopt-a-Dog. I may be a while."

"That's okay. Shawn and I need time to wake up, anyway." She gave her still-sleeping son a tender look.

"Well, if you don't mind waiting. Let me have your paperwork, Kathy. I'll be back soon, I promise."

Deanna stepped outside. The desert sun was still hot and bright, its heat reflected by the bare boulders and rocky pillars jutting out from sparse scrub. Horses, people, stagecoaches and covered wagons seemed to be everywhere.

Deanna headed for the line of people standing in front of a table under a shade tent, certain that was where she needed to check in. Various friends and associates called out her name as she made her way through the crowd. Deanna waved to them, but didn't stop. She needed to get her paperwork done while it was still light.

She hurried forward, her steps causing little dust clouds to rise from the sandy soil. Then she hesitated, wondering if it would be safer to circumvent the equine and wagon traffic and take the long way around. It was obvious that this many unfamiliar horses in a strange area was making all the animals nervous.

Deanna had just decided to take the safer way when someone screamed. She looked up to see two horses attached to a buckboard rearing wildly while an elderly man tried desperately to control them. Then someone else began to scream and people were running away in all directions as the horses touched ground briefly before rearing again.

"Throw the brake!" Deanna yelled to the buckboard driver. "Throw the brake!" But she couldn't be heard above the noise. Picturing the runaway team rampaging through the crowd, she raced toward the pair.

Deanna couldn't believe the throng of people pushing against her, trying to get out of the way. These were horse owners! Why weren't they helping? She shoved hard, forcing her way closer.

The distraught horses were a perfectly matched pair of bays, their black manes and tails a contrast to their brown coats. As Deanna got nearer, she saw they were sweating profusely, the whites of their eyes visible, their nostrils flared. Black hoofs scrambled in the dirt as they frantically sought to escape.

Deanna immediately saw that the brake still hadn't been set as the pair pushed the buckboard backward a few feet, then reared high in the air once more. She picked up her pace, only to be roughly pushed aside by a fleeing man. She fought for her balance, but fell to the ground. Deanna swore, not because she was hurt—she wasn't—but because all these horse owners were behaving so foolishly.

From the other side of the buckboard, a man emerged from the crowd. Deanna breathed a sigh of relief as he ran toward the horses. That sigh caught in her throat as the flailing iron-shod hoofs came dangerously close to his head. The man retreated briefly, his Stetson flying through the air.

Deanna gasped. It was J. D. Vaughn! He lunged for the headstall of the nearest horse, then grabbed the other. He was in front of the pair, struggling to control them.

"Set the brake!" he ordered the elderly driver.

"I did! They broke it!" was the shouted reply.

J.D. dug his boots into the ground as the horses tried to break free of his grasp. Deanna saw that there was still a crowd gathered around them, the vehicles and people providing deadly obstacles. There was no way J.D. could hold the horses for long on his own, and no one else was attempting to help him.

A flash of movement, beige against beige, told Deanna why. In the middle of the small open area around the horses was a sidewinder rattlesnake. The snake was coiled in a striking position, frightening both horses and people. With the crowd surrounding the snake, there was no place for it to retreat, no place for it to hide. The same applied to the horses.

Deanna struggled to her feet. There was only one solution. One of the two would have to go, and she sure couldn't move the team. She clenched her fists and cautiously approached the snake. The horses scrambled wildly, momentarily dragging J.D. off his feet. Deanna waited breathlessly until he was on the ground again before forcing herself to concentrate on the snake. As a vet, she'd handled them more than once. The humane society often called her to milk them for their venom, which was used in antidote production. She'd even caught a few herself for the same purpose.

But those times she'd had a long forked stick that trapped the snake's head against the ground and the neck loop that came with it. She'd also had heavy gloves, a burlap bag and a syringe of antidote in her pocket just in case. All she had now was her two bare hands and no other choice. J.D. was strong, but the horses were stronger. He couldn't hold on forever.

Deanna removed the heavy barrette from her hair. She felt J.D.'s gaze on her and looked up. His eyes locked with hers, and he gave her a reassuring nod. Then the horses shifted again, and he was scrambling for his footing. Still, his encouragement helped strengthen her resolve.

She breathed deeply once, then threw her barrette to distract the snake. The rattler struck with lightning quickness, but Deanna was quicker. She grabbed the snake just below the head as it recoiled. The diamonds on the long thick body twisted and writhed as she lifted the snake in the air, its rattles shaking angrily. Deanna supported the coiled weight in her left hand, the triangular head and deadly fangs tightly immobilized by her right.

The crowd gasped, then broke into sudden applause, but Deanna didn't pay any attention. She exhaled the deep breath she'd been holding and backed away from the horses.

That seemed to be the signal for things to return to normal. A couple of men came out of the crowd to help J.D. with the horses. A path was cleared for Deanna, and a helpful woman brought over an empty aluminum garbage can and lid. Ever so carefully, and ever so quickly, Deanna released the snake into the can and clapped on the cover.

"I'll take care of this pest," a red-faced sweating man offered. "One good shot, and he'll make a nice belt for you, darlin.'" He hefted a rifle in his hands.

"Are you insane?" Deanna's voice cracked with strain, and for a moment she thought she was going to be violently sick. She leaned both hands on the lid of the can and fought for control.

Then she felt a steadying arm slide around her waist and heard J.D.'s voice. "The lady already has a belt."

"Another won't hurt. That rattler's vermin!"

"Wrong. That reptile keeps vermin under control. Even if it didn't, shooting it on an animal-rights charity drive doesn't sit right with me."

"Don't be ridiculous!"

"I didn't see *you* offering to help her out," J.D. challenged. The look of disgust he directed toward the other man caused even Deanna to flinch. "Since she took the risk, I'd say any decisions about the snake are hers. Wouldn't you?"

J.D.'s expression frightened Deanna almost as much as the sidewinder had. J.D. waited until the man walked away, then gave her his full attention.

"Deanna, are you all right?" he asked. His face was all concern now, its earlier menace gone. He ignored the stranger who was trying to give him back his Stetson.

She nodded, liking the comfort of his arm around her waist.

"Shall we set this snake free?"

She let go of the can and straightened. "Yes, let's."

"Why don't we carry this can away from the crowd and turn him loose near some rocks?"

"Okay." J.D. continued to hold her by the waist until Deanna added, "You can let go, now. I'm not going to faint."

J.D. released her. "No, I'm sure you aren't." He grinned as he slapped his Stetson back on his head. "Some people think the only good snake is a dead snake. Especially when it comes to poisonous ones."

"Well, I don't. Snakes are an important part of the desert ecosystem." She shivered. "Although I don't think I'd like to do that again anytime soon." She reached for one handle of the aluminum can, then looked up in surprise when J.D. didn't follow suit. The can certainly wasn't heavy, but it was bulky. She'd assumed he'd help her carry it, especially considering its deadly cargo.

"Wait a minute." He hurried back over to where she'd originally spotted the sidewinder and bent over in the dirt. Deanna watched as he picked up something and cleaned it with a tail of his silk shirt. Then he returned to her, neatly tucking his shirt back in the waistband of his jeans.

"Here. Don't forget this."

It was her barrette.

Deanna looked at it in his hand, then stared at the soiled spot midway down his shirt. The man had just wrestled two rearing horses, stood up to a snake-hating gun-toting idiot and now was gallantly presenting her with her barrette. She felt a warm feeling in the pit of her stomach. His kindness was very touching—and totally unexpected.

"Thanks," she managed to say. She even managed a smile as she swept back her long curls and refastened them with the clip. J.D. watched her every move. It wasn't until she reached for the handle once more that J.D. grasped the other and they set off.

When they were away from the crowd, J.D. said, "That was a nice piece of work, Deanna."

"I had to do something! I was afraid that team was going to break loose. Think of the damage they could have done. If it wasn't for you—"

"And you," he interrupted. "Thanks for stepping in to give me a hand. Although you gave me quite a turn, there. Even I don't go around grabbing rattlers with my bare hands."

Deanna carefully stepped over a rock, then lifted the can over a scraggly bush. "I've handled them before."

"But not without the proper tools, I'm sure," J.D. said, his eyes openly admiring.

"No." Deanna felt herself bask in his admiration. "But it's all over now, thank goodness." She sighed, then checked the area. "We might as well stop here. This looks like a good spot."

There were sharp rocky outcroppings among a patch of cacti. No human being would be tempted to venture here.

They laid the can on its side, then J.D. kicked off the lid. As the two of them retreated a safe distance, the snake emerged and headed straight for the protection of the rocks.

"There he goes," J.D. said as he picked up the can. He put the lid on, then turned to her. "That's one lucky snake. And I'm even luckier you were around to save my hide. I'm grateful, Deanna."

He reached for her and pulled her to him. His kiss was a surprise. It was firm, yet gentle—and unhurried. A startled Deanna immediately realized his kiss held more than just gratitude. But before she could react, before she even had a chance to analyze her own response, he'd set her free again.

"You and I should be heading back," he said, lifting the can and tucking the whole thing sideways under his arm as if nothing had even happened. "We still have to sign in."

"You?" Deanna was confused. The excitement of the snake and spooked horses, then the shock of his kiss, had driven the obvious question out of her mind. "What in the world are you doing here, anyway?"

His eyes twinkled with amusement. "Right to the point. I always liked straight shooters, Deanna. But I think a little more courtesy toward a generous sponsor wouldn't hurt."

"Generous sponsor..."

"Yep. I seem to have developed a sudden soft spot for greyhounds."

Deanna stopped dead. "*You're* the one who pledged all that money to Adopt-a-Dog?"

"A worthy charity. I was shocked to hear about those greyhounds and most grateful your mother filled me in."

Deanna's head spun. "My mother talked to you?" *Again?*

J.D. nodded. "Helen told me how hard you've worked for Adopt-a-Dog. She seemed disappointed that you hadn't acquired many pledges. I hated to see her upset, so..."

"So you pledged a huge amount of money," Deanna finished for him. Suddenly Helen's strange mood made sense. She'd been playing matchmaker again. But Deanna found it difficult to be angry. After all, Helen's efforts *had* benefited Adopt-a-Dog. She ignored the delighted little voice that said it also allowed her to see J.D. again.

"I'm very grateful for your contribution," Deanna said honestly. "I can use all the sponsors I can get. But you still haven't answered my question. What are you doing here?"

J.D. lifted one eyebrow. "Didn't Kathy tell you?"

"Tell me what?"

"I'm coming along for the ride."

CHAPTER FIVE

"KATHY, YOU COULD HAVE told me!" Deanna admonished her friend with a sideways glance into the distance at J. D. Vaughn.

It was the next morning. The wagon train was on its way, the opening ceremonies over and done with. J.D. was riding his horse, and Shawn was in the rear boot atop the stage keeping an eye on Rustler, who was tied to the back. That left Deanna free to sit beside Kathy and discuss the latest developments.

"But Deanna, I told you, I didn't know Mr. Vaughn was coming! I mean, I knew *someone* was coming, but I didn't know it was him!"

"Are you telling me you'd let a perfect stranger ride with you?" she scoffed. "And with Shawn? I know how protective you are of him."

Kathy nodded vigorously. "I am. But my boss from Adopt-a-Horse called me at home. They had a new sponsor who'd offered a big donation to the cause, she said, and he was supposed to ride along with me. It was right before I went to pick you up, Deanna, and I was running late. I didn't get a chance to find out the particulars, and I didn't feel it was necessary. My boss vouched for him, and that was good enough for me, especially since the donation was so large...."

"As large as the one J.D. pledged for Adopt-a-Dog?"

"Almost. Besides, what's the big deal? You couldn't ask for a better sponsor—or trail companion—than J.D. And if he hadn't shown up, who knows what would have happened with that buckboard? I never saw so many people go crazy around a snake," Kathy snorted. "Thank goodness you and J.D. were there."

"I suppose. Still, I wish he'd stayed home."

Kathy was clearly confused. "From my experience dealing with him at Adopt-a-Horse, I know J.D.'s a nice guy. What do you have against him? Any sane woman would appreciate his interest."

Deanna couldn't help but remember the specifics of J.D.'s interest, including the kiss they'd shared yesterday. She stole another look at him. His hand came up to touch the brim of his hat in a silent salute. Deanna gave him a polite nod in return, but refused to let her eyes linger. She also refused to tell Kathy J. D. Vaughn's history with her father.

"You have to watch every step you make around that man," she settled for saying. "Believe me, I know."

"But, Deanna," Kathy said hesitantly, "he must really like you. After all, he pledged a lot of money just because your mother told him you hadn't gotten many sponsors for the greyhounds."

"It isn't the greyhounds he cares about. It's Rustler."

"Rustler?" This time it was Kathy's turn to steal a glance at J.D. "But you told me Rustler was lame."

"*Slightly* lame, but his bloodlines are excellent. He can't be raced, but his offspring could. J.D. would have to put his plans to break into Thoroughbred racing back four years, but I bet he'd do it for Rustler."

"Four years?"

Deanna nodded. "Eleven months for gestation, then two more years before Rustler's offspring were old enough to race in lesser track events. Three for the big-money races. The Triple Crown races—Kentucky Derby, Preakness, Belmont—are only for three-year-olds.''

"I didn't know you knew so much about racing," Kathy said with surprise.

"I know enough to realize that J.D. needs a Thoroughbred stallion bad.''

"Bad enough to donate so much money to charity? From the size of his pledges, he can certainly afford to simply buy another stallion.''

"He could, but he's set his mind on Rustler. He owns and races Rustler's dam, you see. Supposedly that mare is money in the bank.''

"And he's certain Rustler would be, too?''

"Something like that. I wish he'd just stick to quarterhorse racing, or at least leave me and Rustler out of his Thoroughbred expansion plans,'' Deanna grumbled.

"I thought quarter horses were mostly ranch and rodeo horses,'' Shawn piped up from the rear of the stage. "I didn't know they made good racers.''

"They are. But in their own way, they're just as fast as Thoroughbreds,'' Deanna explained. "The strain was originally bred to work cattle. Quarter horses had to be able to run flat out for a good quarter of a mile in order for stockmen to rope escaping cattle.''

"So that's why they're named quarter horses?''

"Yes. With their explosive starts and high bursts of speed, a good quarter horse can outrun a Thoroughbred over short distances. Thoroughbreds were bred for running longer distances.'' Deanna frowned. "Unfortunately quarter-horse racing profits are nowhere near as high or prestigious as Thoroughbred stakes. And that's why J. D. Vaughn is on this trip.''

Both women were silent for a while as the stagecoach bumped along the rocky path.

"Well, I can't hide from him all day. I'm not going to change my mind about Rustler no matter what J. D. Vaughn says."

"That's the spirit, Deanna. After all, we'll be on this Butterfield stage line for a week."

On the line with J. D. Vaughn for a whole week. Despite a vow to remain unaffected, Deanna shivered. She suspected that the man was more than a threat to Rustler. He was also a threat to her.

"We'll be making a stop soon. I'll ride Rustler, and you can have Shawn in front again." Deanna smiled ruefully. "He'll be better company for you than me, I'm sure."

"Hey, if I'd picked up a rattlesnake yesterday the way you did, I'd still be edgy myself. And you could be wrong about J.D.," Kathy said with a shrug. "Maybe he's crazy about you, and this will be the most romantic week of your life."

"And maybe Rustler will sprout wings like Pegasus. Still, I promise not to complain anymore—not to you, anyway."

"Time to take the bull by the horns?"

"Something like that. Did you know he offered me a job as vet on his ranch? Shows you how badly he wants Rustler."

"Rustler—or you."

"Get a grip!" But Deanna wasn't really angry. "Next time we stop, let me off."

Kathy obliged. Soon afterward Deanna was seated on Rustler, loosely sandwiched between Kathy's stage and J.D. and his mount.

"Good morning, Deanna," he greeted her. "I hope you slept well."

"Well enough," she replied, adjusting her hat against the fierce Arizona sun. Despite the earliness of the hour, it was hot under the clear turquoise sky, with little vegetation, not even much cactus, to cool the earth.

"Shawn and I stayed up and talked awhile," J.D. said, moving his horse closer to hers. The intricate Mexican designs of his hand-tooled tack's hanging silver fetishes chimed at the motion. "I was teaching him some of the constellations."

"Yes, I heard you." As soon as she'd spoken, Deanna wished she could take back the words.

"I would have thought you'd be resting up for today. Were you eager for some company?"

She immediately squashed that idea. "Not really. But sound carries far at night."

The party of four had all slept out in the open—men on one side of the stage, women on the other. The stage was far too stuffy inside for anyone to sleep in comfort. Tents had been packed, but rain was sparse in the spring, so the tents had remained untouched.

"As long as I didn't disturb your sleep."

Deanna threw him a quick glance, then decided not to reply. Discretion was certainly the better part of valor in this case, especially since his nearness had kept her awake for most of the night.

And in the full daylight, his magnetism was even harder to resist. He was dressed in his usual outfit of designer jeans and silk shirt—pale green this time—and fancy boots. The huge silver-and-turquoise belt buckle and watch were the same, and of course he wore his Stetson.

Deanna decided to choose a much safer topic than his ability to disturb her. "That's a fine horse you're riding," she said. The palomino gelding's gold coat and creamy mane and tail shone with a glossiness that spoke of frequent grooming.

"Thanks. Pistol Pete here can outlast any horse I've ever had on the trail. I bought him dirt cheap at an auction. Best money I've ever spent."

"What was wrong with him?" She couldn't detect any defects in the horse's build or gait.

"He had an alarming tendency to run away with his riders. All he needed was some patience, some bribery in the form of carrots and a well-fitted curb bit. Worked wonders."

Deanna watched the smooth rippling gait of his mount. "He looks like an easy ride."

"Thanks to his bit, he is. Unlike your horse." J.D. had apparently noticed Rustler's penchant to pull at the bit. "It must hurt your shoulders after a while."

"I can handle Rustler just fine," Deanna said heatedly. "And I don't believe in curb bits. I think they're inhumane."

"Some of them are. But not all of them. You need one that's very carefully fitted, so it'll control, not injure. Pete here has a custom-made brass bit. The brass tastes better and keeps his mouth more moist than plain iron. And there's a brass roller bar in the middle that Pete loves to spin around with his tongue."

Deanna lifted her chin. Roller bars were small textured balls that were mouth toys for horses. They helped to alleviate boredom and distract the animals from the heaviness of the curb bit. But they were frightfully expensive.

"Not all of us can afford custom-made tack. Besides, I don't feel it's necessary."

J.D. gave her a tolerant smile. "Well, you're the vet. I'm just a dumb ex-cowboy. But I'd rather spend a few extra dollars for a curb bit than see a horse or rider end up injured. Especially when the horse is mine, and I'm the rider."

"I'm all for safety. I just don't think Rustler needs a curb bit."

"He's a hell of a lot of horse and still filling out." J.D. studied the stallion carefully, his gaze sweeping from the large intelligent head down to the deep chest and powerful chestnut flanks. "He'll be more than sixteen hands by the time he's mature, if he isn't that already. I'd hate to see you turn into another Mrs. Foley with her barbed-wire-charging gelding."

Deanna bristled at the rebuke but held her temper. "That's not likely," she replied with a chilly look, which didn't quell J.D. in the least.

"Being a vet might mean you know all about equine physiology and how to treat their ailments. However, being a vet *doesn't* mean you know everything about tack, riding and general horsemanship. You obviously don't know a thing about curb bits. I guarantee you Rustler needs one."

"I don't think so. And when it comes to Rustler, I make the decisions."

J.D. shrugged at her tart words. "Suit yourself. I know you have courage, Dr. Leighton. Too bad you're a little short in the horse-sense department."

Fuming, Deanna remembered his own courage of the day before and reminded herself of his generosity toward Adopt-a-Dog. Those two things enabled her to count to ten and keep her cool. She even managed to say, "Perhaps we should agree to disagree and leave it at that."

The rest of the morning passed slowly. The first leg of the Butterfield Trail wound down though Doubtful Canyon and into the San Simon Valley. The descent was fairly easy on the single and draft horses alike. Soon the scenery began to change from barren rocky hills to desolate rocky flats covered with a little more vegetation.

It was hardly the kind of view that would jolly Deanna into a better frame of mind. To make matters worse, her shoulders were beginning to ache from fighting Rustler, just as J.D. had predicted. Her busy practice allowed little time for long horseback rides, which meant she'd never noticed the problem before. But now the sights and smells of new territory and strange horses made the young stallion frisky. Deanna's muscles knotted painfully as she tried to keep him under control.

By the time the twenty-five wagons and the other riders on horseback stopped for lunch, Deanna was stiff and sore. It was an effort just to dismount and picket Rustler among the scrub to forage for food. But she managed to be polite to J.D. and was almost cheerful to the others.

"Are you okay?" J.D. asked when Kathy and Shawn left to chat with some of the other participants.

"Just a little stiff." Deanna barely managed to smile up at him from where she sat on the ground. "I'm not used to riding so much."

"You're one of those all-work-and-no-play kind of people, I gather," J.D. said with a shake of his head. "Wait here. I'll get you some aspirin."

"*You* carry aspirin?"

"Never know when you're going to get thrown. I'm not one of those men who lie and say they never do. That's just tempting fate." J.D. grinned. "I'll only be a minute."

He hurried back from the stage with two tablets and his canteen. "Here. Take these."

Deanna gratefully did. "Thanks. I should have thought to bring some myself. But I guess I'm one of those people you talked about. I never pictured myself getting saddle sore."

He studied her obviously painful movements for a moment, then said, "It's going to be a long afternoon and an even longer week. Would you like to trade horses for the day?"

Deanna's heart sank at that oh-so-casual question. He knew what Rustler had done to her. Her act hadn't fooled him a bit. She ducked her head and busied herself with capping the canteen.

"I know some people don't take kindly to strangers riding their mounts. If you want," he continued nonchalantly, "we could always switch bits."

Deanna closed her eyes and wished the ground would open up and swallow her. Next he was going to say, "I told you so." And she'd have to sit there and take it. What was it about the Leighton family that caused them to always be bested by this man?

Eyes still closed, Deanna admitted to herself the ground wasn't about to comply. She might as well swallow her pride and accept her punishment.

All thoughts of punishment vanished as Deanna felt his hands on her shoulders. Her eyes flew open in astonishment. She made an involuntary move away, then froze as she felt a knot in her muscles relax under his touch, followed by another and another. The feel of his fingers was heavenly.

"There," J.D. said with satisfaction after a couple of minutes. "Better?"

Deanna tentatively lifted her arms. Her shoulders still ached, but at least she could move them again. "Much. Thank you."

"My sister used to get sore shoulders from roping cattle. Sierra would rather die than admit she was hurting. Or ask for help. She was tougher than the rest of us, though.

Kind of like you." J.D. rose from his kneeling position behind her, then extended his hand to help her up.

"I remind you of your sister?" Deanna let him pull her to her feet.

His eyes traveled slowly over her in an appreciative, almost wanton gaze. "Well," he drawled, "not exactly."

Deanna pulled her hand out of his, but she couldn't ignore his boldness. "You do like to push your luck, don't you?"

J.D.'s eyes twinkled. "So I've been told."

"I don't take kindly to being pushed. However, I *can* admit when I'm mistaken. You were right about Rustler. I never rode him long enough to realize it before," she confessed.

J.D.'s expression was one of approval. "Then why don't we switch horses for the day? Tonight I'll make the necessary adjustments to our bridles, and you can ride Rustler tomorrow. You'll be surprised what a difference the curb bit makes."

"Thank you for the offer. I'd be most grateful."

J.D. looked up as the wagon master sounded his horn. "I guess it's time to leave. I'll go get our mounts. You rest those shoulders a bit longer."

"I'm not dying, for heaven's sake," Deanna replied sharply. "I'll go with you."

"I'd like that." His finger tapped her bottom lip ever so briefly. The amusement in his eyes had been replaced by something else. The last time Deanna had seen that look was right after they'd released the snake—and right before he'd kissed her.

Deanna's courage failed her, and she sat back down. "I've changed my mind," she said. Then, when he left to get their horses, she decided sourly that her charms weren't enough to tempt him to insist. She was more perturbed to find that she felt insulted, even though she wasn't eager for more of his attentions. Or was she?

"I'm glad you two are getting along better."

Deanna jumped at the sound of Kathy's voice. "Don't sneak up on me like that!"

"With this pleasingly plump body? Deanna, I never sneak." Kathy watched J.D. retrieve both horses, then turned toward her friend. "He sure seems sweet on you."

"You mean sweet on Rustler."

"No, *you*. I can spot a male interested in a female a mile away. And, honey, that man is interested."

Deanna actually wished the words were true, but she wasn't about to admit it to Kathy. "Now you sound like my mother."

"Maybe because we're both right."

"Ha! If that's true, then why is he going to ride Rustler for the rest of the day?"

Kathy's face was a picture of astonishment. "He's only after a ride on Rustler? That's not very romantic."

"I *told* you he wasn't interested in me," Deanna said, feeling slightly guilty at not telling Kathy the whole story. But then she'd have to confess that J.D. had given her aspirin for sore shoulders and a massage, then offered to switch horses to relieve the stress on her. Who knows what crazy conclusions her romantic friend would jump to?

No, it was better to let the half-truth go unexplained—at least for now.

"Don't feel bad," Deanna told Kathy. "We all can't be as lucky with men as you."

"I wasn't lucky. I was smart enough to return my husband's interest. Something you don't seem to be doing. Giving eligible men like Mr. Vaughn the cold shoulder is just plain crazy."

"I'm being very nice to him." Deanna said evenly. "I'm sure Mr. Vaughn will have no complaints about my company. But please don't play matchmaker. I get enough of that at home."

"I'm sorry. I'll try not to." Kathy's long face made Deanna feel even guiltier.

Her mood wasn't any better as she mounted J.D.'s palomino. Pistol Pete was such an easy ride Deanna could have slept on him without any trouble. The contrast between the gelding and her stallion was appalling and showed her just how much Rustler still had to learn. And how much Deanna still had to teach him. She felt foolish and ignorant. Obviously book learning didn't necessarily make a horsewoman.

Now J. D. Vaughn, there was a horseman. Rustler went through his full bag of tricks with J.D. and soon learned he'd met his match. J.D. was gentle, but firm, never allowing Rustler to get away with anything more than once. The stallion went from irritation to anger to resignation. Eventually his good mood returned, along with a healthy dose of respect for his new rider.

The more Deanna watched them, the worse she felt. The Good Book was right about one thing, she decided. "Pride goeth before a fall," and her pride had certainly taken an awful beating today. Not only had she upset her friend by scolding her matchmaking efforts, she'd also been forced to realize that she wasn't much of a horse trainer.

"Are you all right?" J.D. asked.

"I'm okay," Deanna said, roused from her reverie.

"I wonder. You looked so— I don't know. Sad."

Deanna blinked and sat up straighter in the saddle. "I'm fine. Really."

"Are you sure?"

"I'm a little tired, that's all."

"We'll be stopping at four o'clock to make camp and eat. It's not much longer."

Deanna nodded and looked ahead again. Her mood dampened even further at the sight of the bleak landscape, the clouds of dust thrown up by the wagons and the naked glare of the sun off the rocks.

"Look, I have some more aspirin if your shoulders are still bothering you," J.D. offered. "It won't take but a second for me to get. They're in Pete's pack."

Deanna turned back toward him, surprised by the concern in his voice. The concern was mirrored on his face, but was he really worried about her? She chose her next words carefully.

"You needn't act so nice to me just because you're interested in Rustler," she said quietly.

"Is that what you think I'm doing?"

"Isn't it? First you offer to buy my horse. I refuse, so you offer me a job—to soften me up, I suppose. When that doesn't work, you show up for this charity drive and give me the red-carpet treatment, complete with flattery, concern and even a kiss in the desert. I've said it once and I'll say it again—no matter what you offer me, I'm not going to sell you Rustler, so—"

"What, Deanna?" His voice was harsh, but Deanna refused to back down.

"So you can just go back to your ranch and save yourself all this trouble."

Deanna gave a start at J.D.'s muffled curse, then flinched as he grabbed Pete's reins and pulled the gelding to a stop. He dismounted, still holding both horses' reins in his hand, and approached her. For a second Deanna seriously wondered if she'd gone too far, but then J.D. yanked open one of Pete's saddlebags. She watched him shake out two more aspirin, then silently pass them to her.

He waited until she'd swallowed them with water from his canteen before mounting again, but he still hadn't released her reins. Nor had the anger faded from his face.

"Let me make myself clear, Dr. Leighton. In view of your obvious physical discomfort, your father's past dealings with my ranch and my legitimate need for another vet, I've tried to make allowances for your insults." He gave her a black look. "But my patience is wearing thin. Let me make one thing clear. I'm not going back to my ranch until I'm good and ready!"

"Just as long as you realize you won't be taking Rustler with you. And as for me being your vet, forget it."

"You're turning me down?" he said incredulously.

"That's right. I suggest you look elsewhere." She ignored the twinge of regret that saying goodbye to all the money she could have earned gave her, then hardened her heart. Even if she did take on J.D.'s horses, she'd probably only shorten the time needed to pay back the courts by a few months, anyway.

J.D. jerked his hat back from his face. "You're an even bigger fool than your father!"

Deanna met his steely gaze with one of her own. "I don't think so. You see, I'm smart enough to run the other way when I see trouble."

To prove her point, Deanna urged her horse faster. To her frustration, J.D. immediately did the same, keeping pace.

Suddenly Deanna was tired of his lies, tired of the trail dust and tired of her mind going around and around in circles. She saw that the ground wasn't very rocky here at all and decided a quick gallop wouldn't hurt. Pete could stretch his legs a bit, and she could make her escape.

Deanna kicked Pete's side with her heels. The palomino exploded forward, leaving J.D. and Rustler behind. She heard J.D. call, "I'm not through talking to you!" but ignored him.

The wind rushed through her hair as she enjoyed the sheer freedom of being astride a galloping horse. She could hear Rustler's hoofbeats getting closer, and she urged Pete faster. Her hat flew off, but she still didn't check her progress.

Suddenly Rustler was behind her. Then beside her. There were only four wagons ahead until the front of the train, but Deanna couldn't hold her lead. She saw Rustler's muscles bunch and extend with an awesome power, even though J.D. didn't appear to be urging him on.

Man and horse swept by in a blur. Deanna lost the impromptu race by two full lengths.

In silent accord, they pulled their horses to a canter, then a trot and finally a cool-down walk far ahead of the wagon train. There was nothing before them but the empty miles of the old Butterfield Trail.

Deanna watched Rustler pull at his bit and prance along energetically. "You won," she said, their argument momentarily forgotten. "Despite my head start, you and Rustler won."

"I wasn't trying to race," J.D. replied. "I was just trying to catch up."

"You did, and then some. I never knew Rustler had it in him. And you're much heavier, too. Bad leg or not, Rustler can run!" Deanna marveled. "How did you make him?"

"I didn't. He ran freely, just for the sheer joy of it. Rustler would have done the same for you. I don't think you've ever really given him the opportunity."

"No, I guess I haven't." Deanna yanked the bandanna from her neck and wiped the dust from her face. "Who would have thought he could go so fast?" Then, realizing the absurdity of that question—for of course J.D. had suspected it all along—she was silent.

For long moments the only sounds were the desert wind and the gentle blowing of two slightly winded horses. Finally Deanna looked up to find J.D. watching her. She saw the dust on his face and noticed his bare neck above the open collar of his silk shirt.

"Here." She offered him her bandanna. After gulping down four of his aspirin, it was the least she could do.

"Thanks." J.D. wiped his face clean, then tied the bandanna around his own neck.

"Hey!"

"I'm sure you have another. Consider it your penalty for losing the race."

Deanna gazed at him warily. "What penalty?"

"In the old days, winning knights were awarded their lady's banner. In this case, I'll have to settle for your bandanna."

She stared at the blue paisley square knotted around his neck. "Don't be ridiculous. It needs a good wash first and, anyway, I'm not your lady. Besides," she said, gesturing toward his silk shirt, "it doesn't fit with your image."

J.D.'s eyes blazed with a fire that made Deanna's pulse race. He rode beside her, allowing their thighs to almost touch, and kept Rustler's head even with the palomino's.

"You're a poor loser, Deanna Leighton. To the victor belong the spoils," he announced, deliberately straightening the triangle over his chest.

It was like waving a flag at a bull. "You won on *my* horse," she reminded him. "And if a dusty bandanna is your idea of spoils, maybe next time you should set your goals a little higher." She lifted her chin defiantly.

"Maybe I will." His hand whipped out to cup the nape of her neck and pull her close. Then he kissed her long and hard—on horseback and in front of the whole wagon train.

"You were right," he announced when he finally released her. "Thanks for the advice."

Deanna stared at him as he whirled Rustler around and rode back to Kathy's stagecoach.

Dear Lord, what had she gotten herself into?

CHAPTER SIX

"ARE YOU AND J.D. having problems?" Kathy called from her perch atop the stage. "You've been awfully quiet this morning."

"We've only been on the trail for half an hour," Deanna said. She sat astride Rustler who, thanks to J.D.'s curb bit, was being very obedient. "I really haven't had a chance to wake up."

Which wasn't exactly a lie. She hadn't slept very well last night. She tried to convince herself it was the strange surroundings, but that *was* a lie. J. D. Vaughn made her far more restless than any Arizona night could.

Kathy's expression grew wise. "You're more than awake, Deanna. I wouldn't think a thirty-year-old woman—"

"I'm twenty-eight!"

"Whatever—would be scared by a kiss. For heaven's sake, Deanna, it was only one time."

"That was *not* the only time," Deanna retorted.

"You mean . . . Oh!"

"Yes. At least the first time he kissed me we were alone. Unlike yesterday, when the whole wagon train got to watch. It appears I'm not safe anywhere."

A delighted Kathy looked over at J.D. who was riding near the front of the wagon train, then turned back to Deanna. "Who in their right mind would want to be safe from the likes of that?"

"Me, for one! There's nothing more insulting than being romanced for my horse. If I wasn't so fond of Rustler, I'd sell him to a good home just to be rid of that man."

"Are you certain J.D.'s only interested in your horse?"

"What else is there?"

"You, of course."

Deanna shook her head at the conviction in Kathy's voice. "I don't think so. I can't trust him."

"Why?"

"Just . . . because."

"That's no reason. Deanna, can't you tell me?"

Suddenly Deanna wanted to talk about it. And to a sympathetic *objective* person, which her mother hardly was. But she couldn't talk about her family's problems with Shawn sitting there. She must have given Shawn some sort of look, because Kathy immediately reacted.

"Shawn, why don't you get down and catch up with Mr. Vaughn for a while?"

Once Shawn was gone, Deanna took in a deep breath, and the whole story came tumbling out.

How Carl had bought a bad racer from J. D. Vaughn. How Carl had swindled both family and shareholders and involved his innocent wife. How Deanna and her mother had been forced to move to Cactus Gulch because of the stigma of Helen's criminal record. How the Leightons were in debt to the courts and were likely to remain that way for a long, long time.

And finally, how she wanted nothing to do with the horse trader who'd dealt with her father.

By the time she finished, Kathy's face was white. "Deanna, I'm so sorry! I had no idea."

"Well, it's not the kind of thing we advertise. And thank you for listening. But now can you understand why I'm nervous around J. D. Vaughn? I have to question his motives."

"He doesn't know about all this?"

"He knows what happened up until my father's death, but not about my mother's arrest or anything that happened after. And I don't *want* him to know. The last thing my mother and I need is pity. It's bad enough he's trying to create a vet job for me at his ranch. Mom and I are doing just fine. I mean, we aren't rolling in money, but we're not in the poorhouse. Kathy, you have to promise me you won't tell him any of this."

"You know I won't, but Deanna, do you mind if I say something?"

"No."

"I've worked at Adopt-a-Horse for ten years. For seven of them J.D. Vaughn's bought horses from us. He's always been honest in his business dealings, both now and back before he started to make it big. I don't think he would have cheated your father, Deanna."

Deanna felt a little of the tension ease about her heart. "Perhaps not. But what about that vet job? How can you say that's not charity?"

Kathy bit her lip. "Well, it does sound like the kind of thing J.D. would do. But you'd earn your money," she insisted. "It wouldn't be a handout."

"Maybe so, but what about J.D.'s preoccupation with Rustler? What about this romantic interest he's suddenly developed in me? You're the one who told me he was quite the ladies' man. Can you honestly say he's not above sweet-talking me into selling Rustler?"

"I don't know," Kathy said after a moment. "That's something you'll have to find out for yourself. And you'll never learn a thing riding next to me, instead of next to him."

"What am I supposed to do? Go up and say, 'Hey, J.D., how much romancing does my prime Thoroughbred get me?'"

"Don't be ridiculous. Just try to get to know the man better. Have a normal conversation with him."

"Normal?" Deanna's voice rose. "I haven't found one topic yet that we can agree on."

"Try talking about early Arizona history. That's your hobby. And J.D. knows something about the early stagecoach days. He was telling Shawn earlier that he did a paper on it during college."

Deanna threw Kathy a speculative glance. "That should be tame enough for both of us."

"That's the spirit. You don't want him to think you're hiding."

"As long as I own Rustler, I doubt there's anywhere in this state I could hide. J. D. Vaughn is the most stubborn man I've ever met."

"Well, he's met his match in you. Send Shawn back to me if you want. And, Deanna..."

"Yes?"

"Try giving J.D. the benefit of the doubt, okay?"

"I'm not making any promises."

Deanna took a steadying breath, then reined Rustler back and around the stage. J.D. saw her and touched the brim of his hat in the now familiar salute. He slowed the palomino until Deanna was riding even with him. Just as she rode up, a group of boys motioned for Shawn to walk with them.

When Shawn had moved away, J.D. said, "Hello, Deanna. Glad to have your company again."

"Hello, J.D." Deanna noticed that her blue bandanna was around his neck, nestling comfortably against the pale blue of his fresh silk shirt. She'd bet her last cent he'd waited all morning for her to see it. She refused to give him the satisfaction of commenting.

"Here's your hat," he said, reaching behind him into his saddlebag. "I went back for it last night."

"Thanks." Deanna moved Rustler closer so she could reach it, but she made certain there was still a good amount of distance between J.D. and her.

J.D. noticed her action and gave her a mocking smile. "Scared, Deanna?"

She smiled sweetly back at him. "Should I be?"

There was no answer to that, and no further conversation for some time. Deanna was determined not to let the day go by in awkward silence, however, so she searched for a particularly bland opening sentence.

"This land is nicer than what we rode through yesterday."

J.D. now seemed eager to talk. "We'll be climbing up to Apache Pass in the Chiricahua Mountains soon. Riding through the juniper and oak forests will be a pleasant change."

Deanna nodded. "We'll be near Cave Creek. I'll be glad to see some real trees again. And feel some real shade."

"Where do we go after that?"

Of course J.D. wouldn't know all the details of the route, Deanna thought. "We'll cross Sulphur Springs Valley and continue on toward Dragoon Springs. We'll stop for the night there. It's green, though not quite as pleasant as Cave Creek. Then it's back to desert."

"Guess that's why the Apaches used the Chiricahuas for one of their strongholds."

"Yeah, they knew the Butterfield stages would stop for water at Cave Creek."

"They raided the stages at other water sources, as well," J.D. immediately corrected. "Since the Apaches were mainly after horses, they allowed the stages to enter their territory."

"That's right. Kathy told me you studied the history of staging."

J.D. shrugged. "I know enough. But I'm from Colorado. You're the native Arizonan. You could probably teach me a thing or two about this leg of the Butterfield Trail."

"Maybe." Deanna seriously wondered if she could teach J.D. anything. He always seemed to be one step ahead of her. "Why don't you tell me what you know, and I'll fill in the details?"

"Okay." He took a swig of water from his canteen, replaced it and patted Pistol Pete's neck before continuing. "Stagecoaching began in California in 1849—the year of the gold rush. James Birch went West to make his fortune driving miners to the gold fields. He was the first to offer regularly scheduled stage service. Others followed, but I'm not sure exactly where Mr. Butterfield came in," he admitted.

"He started out in the mail business back East," Deanna replied. "He was also a personal friend of President Buchanan, so he was able to get the government contract to deliver mail to the West. The contract specified mail delivery from St. Louis to San Francisco in twenty-five days. In September of 1858, Butterfield was granted one year to blaze the trail and begin service."

"That doesn't seem like very long," J.D. said.

"It wasn't. Butterfield had to build 165 stage stations and clear three thousand miles of road. Not to mention acquire horses, mules, stages and hire over 750 men. But Butterfield was determined. Service did start exactly one year later."

"Oh, right. And didn't he end up delivering the mail in less than twenty-four days?"

"Yes. It was such a success that passengers soon joined the mail run. For $200, Butterfield would get you to the gold fields, if the Indians or bad food didn't get you first."

"Don't forget the stage robbers," J.D. added. "They were worse than the Indians. The Apaches only wanted horses, but the robbers wanted gold and hated to leave witnesses. In those days the stages routinely carried anywhere from one-hundred thousand to a quarter of a million dollars in gold. Those were high stakes back then."

"That's a lot of money now."

"Yes, it is. Men soon discovered it was easier to steal gold than mine for it. Wells Fargo alone had an average of over twenty successful stagecoach robberies a year. A good quarter of those went unsolved."

Deanna sighed. "Still those must have been exciting days to live in. First there was the early pioneer staging, then the overland stage routes were established..."

"And then came the railroads."

"Yes. The transcontinental railroad was the end of the stages," Deanna said.

"But not right away. The golden spike was driven in 1869, but stage lines continued to prosper well into the 1880s. The trains brought the settlers West, but stagecoaches still provided the only north-south transportation."

"I didn't know that."

"It's true," J.D. confirmed. "In fact, it wasn't until automobiles arrived that stagecoach service finally died. Whatever happened to the Butterfield line?"

"John Butterfield was a wise man. He saw what was happening with the railroads. He sold out to Henry Wells and William Fargo, and in 1850, he invested in a new company called American Express."

"As in the credit card?"

"That's right. The American Express card is John Butterfield's legacy to modern times."

"Now *that* I didn't know."

"I wasn't trying to top you," Deanna replied lightly in response to his rueful tone of voice.

"No, but I'm still impressed. So, shall we declare a truce?"

A flattered Deanna found that during their conversation her edginess had evaporated.

"Only if you admit I know more about stagecoach history than you do," she said smugly.

"But that may not be true," J.D. protested. "I can even name the legendary stage drivers. Except they were called charlies, jehus or—"

"Whips," Deanna finished for him. "And so can I. Hank Monk was famous for his driving skill. He could turn a six-horse team in the middle of the street at a full run, then stop on a dime."

"Jim Miller—known for his fancy yellow overcoat and yellow pants," J.D. countered. "He wore high-heeled boots, even though he was six feet tall."

"I can beat that. How about Curly Bill? He once pulled an army officer out of his stage for insulting a lady, tearing the whole door off in the process."

"Now that's my kind of man," J.D. said with admiration. "But I've got the topper—Charlie Parkhurst. Do you know about him?"

Deanna desperately tried to place the name.

"Aha, I've got you! Charlie Parkhurst drove for twenty years in California, a long time when you consider the hostile elements along the line. He was credited with shooting at least one stage robber to death, was feared by others and only retired after arthritis crippled his hands."

"The name's vaguely familiar," Deanna said slowly, unwilling to be bested.

"Then you should know that Charlie Parkhurst created a big sensation when he died. Those who found him discovered that he was— Well, Deanna, fill in the rest."

Deanna sighed in exasperation. "I can't."

"A woman. Charlie Parkhurst was a woman."

"A *female* stagecoach driver?" She was amazed. "All right, I concede, but I won't be gracious about it. Trust you to know the more sensational aspects of American history."

J.D. laughed. "Deanna, you do humble me. My sister always said I needed a woman who wasn't impressed by my looks, brains or charm." He looked at her. "She'll be thrilled to know I've finally found her."

"I don't know if that's a compliment or an insult." Deanna silently told herself it meant nothing either way.

"I definitely meant it as a compliment."

"You do?" she said, both surprised and delighted. She studied him carefully; the expression on his face was one she'd never seen before. When he spoke, his voice lacked its usual lightheartedness.

"I've met very few women who can get past appearances. In my rodeo days, they only saw the ribbons and the trophies and the glory of my big wins. Nowadays they only see my fancy racehorses, fancy cars, fancy clothes—" J.D. lifted the collar of his silk shirt, then disdainfully dropped it "—and all are dutifully impressed. But very few of them bother to search for the real me. You, Deanna, are one of those few."

Deanna stared at him, unable to deny the pleasure his words gave her. But not knowing what to say, she pretended to take in the scenery. When she finally had the courage to look at him again, she was pleased to see admiration in his eyes. She was even more pleased that the subject of Rustler hadn't entered the conversation once.

He waited until he had her full attention before saying, "You are some lady, Deanna Leighton."

"Ha! Real ladies aren't the subject of the latest wagon train gossip."

"Ouch. I deserved that. As long as I'm apologizing, I'll make a clean sweep."

"You're sorry you kissed me?" Deanna forced herself to keep her voice even.

"Hell, no. But I'm sorry I kissed you in front of all those wagging tongues. I didn't even consider that. Next time I'll kiss you in *back* of the wagon train."

"In back..." Astounded, she couldn't finish.

J.D. nodded innocently and held up his hand as if he was swearing an oath. "In back of the wagon train, away from all those staring eyes. I promise."

Deanna tried to conjure up a disapproving frown, but her cheeks flushed. Another moment and J. D. Vaughn would win this round hands down.

"I'm going to go check on Shawn," she announced, trying to change the subject.

"But you'll be back?" he asked, his expression welcoming, his eyes hopeful.

It was that hopeful look that finally decided Deanna. "I'll be back," she said firmly.

Then she kicked Rustler into a canter and rode off, afraid that if she stayed any longer, she'd forget that she didn't trust J. D. Vaughn.

"I SEE YOU and J.D. are getting along okay now," Kathy said with satisfaction that night. "Aren't you glad you took my advice?"

The wagon train had stopped near a large grove of trees. Water was nearby, and the barren terrain of earlier had changed to a lush green. The sun had set in a red-orange sky, and a delightful coolness filled the clear Arizona air.

"I certainly am. Thanks to your suggestion, we had a good conversation," Deanna replied, remembering also his flattering comments. "Better yet, he didn't mention buying Rustler once today."

"Then things are looking up," Kathy said happily. "I told you he was a nice guy. Now I know I promised I wouldn't play matchmaker, but there's a sing-along at the main camp fire in a little while. Why don't you come with me? Shawn and J.D. are already there. You could sit next to him."

"Maybe in a bit. I want to check on Rustler first."

"One of these days you'll get your priorities straight," Kathy commented with a wry shake of her head.

Deanna merely shrugged and watched her friend walk off into the darkness. The wagons had pulled into the traditional circle, which had once provided both protection from Indians and a makeshift corral for the horses. Neither was necessary now, but the circle was still formed because of the warmth it created and the socializing it allowed.

Deanna wasn't above the desire for either. However, there was no need to appear eager to be with J.D.—even if she was. She was as yet undecided when it came to J.D.'s motives. She had stopped holding him accountable for selling that horse to her father. But when it came to her and Rustler...

So, a few extra minutes checking on the horses before joining J. D. Vaughn wouldn't hurt. She grabbed a couple of apples from inside Kathy's stagecoach and headed outside the wagon circle to where the horses were picketed.

She checked on J.D.'s palomino and fed him his treat, then went over to Rustler. The stallion gave a soft nicker as she approached. He butted his head against her shoulder, his nostrils flared as he searched for the fruit.

"One sniff, and you have a fit. You're so impatient," she scolded and held out the apple for him. "Just like every other male."

"From the woman who objected to being called a spirited filly, that sounds kind of sexist to me."

Deanna whirled around. J.D. stood there grinning at her.

"It probably is," she said, unable to hide her pleasure at seeing him. "However, I'm not going to take it back."

"Why am I not surprised?" J.D. sat down on a weathered boulder. "I thought you'd be at the camp fire. I looked for you."

"I was going there. I just wanted to check on the horses."

He nodded. Deanna patted Rustler's neck, delighted that J.D. had actually searched for her and wondering what he was thinking. She didn't have to wonder long.

"Actually I'm glad I have you out here all to myself."

Deanna immediately went on her guard. "Is that so?"

"Yes. Come sit next to me." He gestured at the rock. "There's room."

Deanna cautiously joined him, her thigh inches from his as she perched on the boulder. "Well, here I am. You have my undivided attention."

"I'll believe it when you stop checking on the horses," he said dryly. "Don't you ever get tired of playing vet, Dr. Leighton?"

Deanna was startled by the impatient note in his voice, and her breath caught at the look in his eyes. There was no mistaking his intention, no chance to avoid his kiss. Not that she wanted to ...

His arms circled her waist, and his lips covered hers. For the first time, Deanna boldly allowed herself to return the kiss.

When he finally drew away she said, "You promised you wouldn't kiss me unless we were in back of the wagon train."

"Ah, but the wagons are in a circle. So technically we are in back of them. Which means I won't feel at all guilty if I do this." He dropped a light kiss on the corner of one eye. "And this." He did the same to the other. "And this."

He kissed her again on the lips. And when they broke apart she was breathless. Kissing J. D. Vaughn was without a doubt better than a camp fire sing-along.

"You're awfully quiet," he said after a moment, one arm still around her waist. "Are you wondering what I do for an encore?"

"There won't be an encore," Deanna said, but she made no move to leave.

J.D. grinned wickedly. "Are you sure you don't want one?"

"Absolutely," she lied.

He gave a mock sigh. "Then I'll have to offer you something else."

"Something else?"

"Yes. I have some news that'll cheer you up."

"What?" Deanna asked curiously, deciding to skip the camp fire altogether. It was much more pleasant sitting alone in the Arizona night with J. D. Vaughn.

"It's about Rustler."

"Rustler?" Deanna was jolted out of her pleasant lassitude and she stiffened. "What about him?"

"I've ridden him and watched him when you've ridden him. It's about that limp of his."

Deanna felt the romance of the moment slipping inexorably away.

"When Rustler is running he doesn't limp. And when he was wearing the curb bit and playing with the roller bar, he didn't limp then, either. Didn't you notice?"

"I... Come to think of it," she said slowly, "his gait was a lot smoother."

"There's a reason for that. You know how sometimes a cough lingers when you get a bad cold? Long after you feel better?"

"Yes."

"That's because the body has gotten into the habit of coughing. Even though the virus is gone, the body continues to cough. It's the same thing with Rustler's limp."

Deanna bit her lip. Could he be right? She knew his theory was medically sound, and she also knew how wise he was about horses.

"What are you saying?" she asked, carefully enunciating each word.

"I'm saying that Rustler has nothing physiologically wrong with him. His limp is just a habit, something he does when he's bored. I've seen similar patterns in other horses. Some will occasionally kick, others will play with their tails. Or... Well, you get the picture."

Deanna nodded mutely.

"And Deanna, you're too busy to give Rustler enough attention. I'd stake my reputation that his tendons are sound. And if his X rays are clean..."

"They are." Deanna's heart sank.

"There you go!"

"So, what you're saying is..." Not for the life of her could she finish, or fight against the painful suspicion that filled her.

"Your stallion isn't lame!" J.D. announced triumphantly. "Rustler is prime racehorse material! Isn't that good news?"

CHAPTER SEVEN

"YOUR STALLION isn't lame! Isn't that good news?" The words echoed over and over again in Deanna's head.

"Good news?" she choked out. "For who? Me or you?"

"I thought you'd be happy, Deanna."

"Happy? Happy that I've been foolish enough to believe you were attracted to me?" She jumped off the rock and stared at him. "Happy to know you were only interested in Rustler all along?"

"Deanna, don't be ridiculous." J.D. reached for her arm, but she shook him off.

"I don't hear you denying it!" she yelled. "Prime racehorse material, indeed. Well, I'm a prime idiot! I've been kissed by men before, but never have I come second to a horse! And I'm not about to start, any more than I'm going to sell you Rustler." Deanna felt as if she'd been kicked in the head—or was it her heart?

"This has *nothing* to do with me buying Rustler! It's about his being healthy. I thought you'd be excited. I thought you'd want to know."

"Not while you were kissing me!" Deanna was livid—at him and at herself. "But of course, you weren't really romancing me, were you?"

J.D.'s eyes were unreadable. "Wasn't I?"

"No. You were just using me to get to Rustler. Well, your technique leaves a lot to be desired."

His expression hardened at her insult. "I didn't hear you complaining."

"Well, I'm complaining now!" She stomped back toward the camp. "And I certainly don't intend to repeat the experience! Good night!"

Only it wasn't a good night. It was a miserable sleepless night, followed by a miserable cheerless morning. It was a subdued Deanna who sat on Rustler after sunrise, although she made sure she rode on the side of the stage opposite J.D.

"What's wrong?" Kathy asked.

"I'm hot and cranky," Deanna replied. That was partly the truth, for the trail had taken them away from the cool trees. They were now back in the dry parched desert.

"So am I." Kathy fanned her face with her hat. "Thank goodness we won't be riding anymore after lunchtime. I could use a break from this heat myself."

By noon there would be no trail left. Originally it had followed Cienaga Creek to Tucson, but the city and its outlying suburban areas had absorbed the old trail. Arrangements had been made for the horses and wagons to be picked up and transported north of Tucson. The charity drive would resume just past Picacho Peak.

"Are you going to be okay until then?" Kathy asked with concern.

After what happened last night?

"I'll manage." Deanna gritted her teeth. "I've been through tougher spots than this."

"That's the spirit. Why don't you go talk to J.D. again? Maybe he can take your mind off your troubles."

"He *is* the trouble," she grumbled, but not wanting J.D. to think her a coward, she rode to the other side of the stage.

"I wondered if I'd see you today," J.D. remarked as she pulled abreast of him.

"As you're a sponsor and I'm here in my official capacity as vet, I see no reason why we can't act like civilized adults."

"I see. So, no sulking or silent treatment?"

"Not from me." Deanna refused to show him how much she'd been hurt last night. "I prefer polite conversation, unless *you* prefer to act the injured party." Seeing his eyebrows knit together Deanna knew she'd annoyed him and was perversely glad.

"There's always staging history for a safe topic," he said.

"If you wish." Deanna sat stiffly erect on Rustler. "We can talk about Kathy's Concord, the Cadillac of all stagecoaches."

"Fine," he retorted. "For starters, you can tell me where Kathy got her replica."

"The stage belongs to Adopt-a-Horse. They use it for publicity. Kathy knows how to drive both a four-team and six-team hitch, and so does Shawn. They also know how to be pleasant trail companions," she couldn't help adding.

J.D. shot her a black look. "The Concord coach was made by Abbott-Downing in New Hampshire, and at least Kathy and Shawn aren't paranoid."

Deanna drew an indignant breath. "Lewis Downing copied the shape from the old English coach and added his own refinements. They were painted red with black leather boots and straps, yellow wheels and running gear. I doubt Kathy's husband ever kissed her with ulterior motives."

J.D.'s face hardened even more. "Concords cost fifteen hundred a coach, the highest in the nation because of their leather shock absorbers. Other vehicles had none. And I'll bet Kathy concentrates on kissing her husband back, instead of trying to look for ulterior motives."

Deanna gasped, unable to believe the nerve of the man! "The coaches were made in three sizes, could hold six to nine passengers inside and nine to twelve on top. Believe me, Mr. Vaughn, you've made no secret of your motives from the first day I met you. Finesse certainly isn't your strong point."

J.D.'s fingers clenched the reins tightly. "Concord coaches were shipped all over the world, including Mexico, South America, Africa and Australia. My being interested in Rustler is no reason I can't also be interested in you!"

Deanna tossed her head defiantly. "Abbott-Downing held the corner on the market, much to the cattlemen's delight. It took twelve to fourteen ox hides to make one coach's leather boots and shock absorbers. And you're crazy if you think I intend to let any man lump me together with a horse! I'm part of nobody's package deal!"

"I never said that!"

"Too bad you didn't," Deanna spat out. "At least then I'd be getting equal billing. Thank goodness I had the sense to turn down your little charity job."

"Is that what you thought my job offer was? Charity?"

"Or bribery."

There was a deadly silence. "If you were a man, Deanna Leighton, I'd break your damn neck."

"Go right ahead and try. I'll give you a run for your money." Her words were bitterly flung back with more than just injured pride or hurt feelings. There was a deeper emotion, a knowledge that—whether she liked it or not— J.D. meant more to her than she cared to admit. "But you still won't get Rustler."

"I'm not used to having my integrity questioned," he said in a voice that sent chills down her spine. "And if I didn't know about you and your mother—"

He broke off abruptly as Deanna turned to stare at him accusingly. "If you didn't know *what* about us?" she demanded.

"If I didn't know about your father's history with the racing business, I wouldn't sit here listening to your insults."

"Don't do me any favors!"

"I won't!" J.D. reined Pete hard to the side, and within seconds Deanna was riding alone. The trail seemed desolate and empty with his departure. She longed to go after him, but knew there was no point. She couldn't say what he wanted to hear—that she trusted him.

She couldn't afford to. It wasn't just the ownership of her stallion that was on the line.

It was also her heart.

THE WAGON TRAIN STOPPED outside of Tucson a few hours later. Deanna climbed off Rustler and picketed him, trying to avoid seeing J.D., but seeing him, anyway. He looked angry and unapproachable. Deanna shivered and busied herself helping Shawn and Kathy load the horses and stage into Adopt-a-Horse's waiting trucks.

"I thought you said your husband was going to pick up your truck and drop it off here," Deanna said to Kathy when the last of the team was inside the trailer. "I don't notice it anywhere. I need to load Rustler." There was no room for him in any of Adopt-a-Horse's trailers.

"It's here, but I forgot to tell you. My husband took the horse trailer back home and just left me the truck. You can load Rustler in J.D.'s trailer."

"J.D.'s?" Deanna squeaked.

"Yes. He already said it was okay. I knew you wouldn't mind."

"But—" Deanna stole a glance at J.D. Sure enough, he'd already put the palomino into his double trailer and was busy unsaddling Rustler.

"You're riding with him, too."

"Riding with him? As in, up to the Picacho Peak trail?" Kathy nodded. "You're really better off. Some of Shawn's friends want to come with us. You can keep J.D. company while I ride with a bunch of noisy teenagers. Just tell him the way to the next stop. He'll get you there in plenty of time." Kathy glanced at her watch. "I've got to go, Deanna. I want to get something to eat in town, and I need to use a phone before we leave. See you at Picacho Peak."

"Okay. 'Bye." She watched Kathy flutter her hand, then resolutely squared her shoulders and headed toward J.D.'s trailer.

"I can do that," Deanna offered as J.D. finished stripping Rustler's back of blankets and started to lead him into the trailer.

"I'll do it. If you want to help, put your tack in the box up front. It's unlocked."

Deanna hated the curtness in his voice, but did as instructed. She carefully stowed the saddle, blankets and bridle in the trailer's storage area. By the time she was done, J.D. had loaded Rustler and secured the rear door.

"Kathy told you that you were coming with me?"

"Yes, she did."

"Then let's get going. We don't have all day." He opened the passenger door of the truck, which had the Rocking J logo on it, and watched her get in.

"Thank you," Deanna said.

J.D.'s only reply was a taciturn look and a slam of the door. Deanna sighed. It was going to be a long ride to Picacho Peak.

They started out in silence, then J.D. asked her if she needed to stop in Tucson.

"Please," she said. "I'd like to call my mother. And we should probably get something to eat."

"If you like."

His tone was colder than his air-conditioned truck. Deanna miserably counted the minutes until J.D. pulled off the main highway and onto the busy streets of Tucson.

"There's a phone at this gas station. Will it do?" he asked.

"That'll be fine."

He pulled the truck and horse trailer into the full-serve lane of gas pumps, then climbed out. "Fill it up and check the oil, please," he told the attendant. "The keys are still in the ignition. The key to the gas cap is the little silver one."

The attendant nodded. J.D. opened Deanna's door, then gestured toward the outdoor pay phone.

"I'll meet you back at the truck. Do you have enough change?" he asked with studied politeness.

"Yes, thank you," she said, just as politely. Judging by the pulsing vein in his neck, he still wanted to throttle her. She watched as he walked over to the cashier's booth, debated going after him, then stopped when he grabbed the oversize key to the men's room from the wall. She moved away to make her phone call.

She dialed the clinic's number, looking forward to hearing a friendly voice. But the phone rang and rang. Frowning, she pressed the hook, picked up her change and reinserted it. Maybe she'd dialed the wrong number.

This time she punched in the number carefully. Again no answer and, puzzled, she hung up. The clinic occasionally got extremely busy, but Helen usually managed to pick up the phone, or at least leave the answering machine on.

She was gathering up her change when the sudden start of J.D.'s truck engine caught her attention. Surely he wouldn't leave without her.

"Hold your horses," she muttered. "I'm coming." She took a few steps toward the truck, then froze. The change in her hand fell to the oil-stained concrete. The truck was driving away, but J.D. wasn't the driver!

"J.D.!" she screamed. "J.D., come quick!"

But he was nowhere to be found. In desperation, Deanna started running after the truck. But it was an exercise in futility. After a few blocks the speeding truck turned down a busy side street and disappeared.

Deanna stood stock-still in the middle of a crowded sidewalk, watching the cars and people go by. Her heart was pounding like a trip-hammer, and she gasped for air, trying to catch her breath. She was perilously close to collapsing or bursting into tears. Or both.

Think! she told herself fiercely. *Get yourself under control.* She concentrated on taking deep breaths, ignoring the stares of curious onlookers. *I need J.D. We have to find the truck. And Rustler. And Pistol Pete.*

"Deanna! Deanna, where are you?"

Deanna glanced down the sidewalk to see J.D. shoving people aside in his haste to find her.

She couldn't answer, but when she waved he saw her. Then he was at her side, his arms tight around her, his face close to hers. "My God, are you all right?"

Deanna blinked. Was this J.D.? She barely recognized his voice.

"Answer me! Are you hurt?"

She shook her head, then clutched at his shirt in an effort to control her shaking. J.D. must have felt her tremors because he held her even tighter.

"What happened?"

She tried to speak, but her words were unintelligible. She took in a few more gulps of air, then said two words.

"What was that, sweetheart?" J.D. asked. "I couldn't hear."

Did he actually call me sweetheart? Deanna cleared her throat and tried again. "Horse thieves." This time the words came out clearly. "Right in the middle of downtown Tucson!" she added in disbelief.

"But you're okay?"

"Didn't you hear me? The horses are gone! Stolen!"

"Are . . . you . . . okay?" he repeated slowly.

Deanna was startled to see how pale he was. "I told you I was," she said in a more normal voice. She felt his body relax somewhat against hers.

"Tell me everything," he ordered.

"I was making my phone call and I heard the truck start. I thought it was you, so I hurried back. But it wasn't you at all."

"You got a good look at the driver?"

"No," Deanna said miserably. "I could only tell that he was shorter than you and had on a baseball cap. I called you. . . ."

"I heard," J.D. tersely admitted.

"But you didn't come, so I chased after the truck and—"

"You idiot! That thief could have been dangerous! Even armed!" J.D. shook her hard. "What were you going to do if you caught up to the truck? Grab the bumper and stop it with your bare hands?"

"I didn't think!"

"You sure as hell didn't!" J.D. almost shook her again, but restrained himself.

"I just— J.D., the Mexican border isn't far! If he smuggles the horses into Nogales, we'll never see them or your truck again!"

"I know." J.D.'s expression wasn't pleasant. "Let's go back to the gas station and call the police. Whoever took the truck can't drive that fast hauling two horses. That's one thing in our favor. Have you caught your breath? Can you walk?"

"Yes, I'm fine."

J.D. slung his arm around Deanna's waist. This time she didn't hesitate to put her arm around his and keep it there, all the way to the gas station.

The police responded quickly and took down the information.

"Bad luck with those keys, Mr. Vaughn. Shame you don't pump your own gas. And worse luck to be in the men's room when the thief showed up."

"It wasn't *his* fault!" Deanna instantly leapt to his defense. "Maybe if you'd start looking for the truck, instead of blaming J.D. we'd get some results!"

"Deanna, please," J.D. murmured, placing a comforting hand on her arm. "They're right. It *was* bad luck."

"So where can we contact you folks?" the officer asked. "You aren't local."

"I'll give you my sister's number. She lives near Apache Junction—that's fairly close."

"And where will you be after you fill out the paperwork?"

"I'll hang around the police station awhile, in case there's some word. I can get a hotel for the night if I have to." J.D. turned to Deanna. "Shall I get you a cab? You can get back to Kathy and the wagon train."

Deanna's jaw dropped. "Are you crazy?"

"There aren't any phones there, Deanna," J.D. said patiently. "Kathy will be worried when we don't show up."

"I don't care! Rustler's my horse. I'm staying here with you."

The policeman looked at her compassionately. "You might want to take your boyfriend's advice, miss, and go. If the thief's crossed the border...well, you know what the economy's like in Mexico. They'll sell your horse to anyone they can find, and no one will be the wiser." Deanna felt her face go white. "They wouldn't even ask for registration papers?"

"I'm afraid not," the officer said sympathetically. "And the Mexican police aren't much help when it comes to tracing stolen cars. Once a vehicle crosses the border, you can pretty much write it off."

"I'm not leaving until J.D. does. That's final."

The officer nodded. "If that's what you want. I'll give you both a ride to the station to fill out the paperwork. Come with me."

If the drive into Tucson with J.D. had been miserable, this ride was sheer hell. However, Deanna somehow managed to remain calm. At the station she managed to sign all the papers with steady fingers and even fetched J.D. a cup of coffee from the vending machine without spilling a drop. Then she made another attempt at calling her mother. This time the answering machine picked up, and Deanna left a message that ended on a falsely confident note. But as darkness fell without a word, Deanna's courage began to evaporate.

It was almost a relief when J.D. said, "It doesn't look like there's anything else we can do here, Deanna. Let's find a hotel."

"SHALL I CALL room service and order something to eat?" he asked while unlocking the door to her room. His was next door. "We missed lunch and dinner."

"You go ahead." Deanna went in and sank despondently onto the bed. "I'm not hungry."

"Neither am I. I'd probably choke on it." J.D. sat in the room's only chair and studied her carefully. "You aren't going to cry, are you?"

"I'm thinking about it."

"If you get to cry, I get to punch my fist through a wall," J.D. warned. "Or put my foot through the door."

"You wouldn't!"

"I'm thinking about it," he replied, echoing her words. "I swear I am. They got my horse too."

Deanna saw he was serious. "I won't if you won't."

"Deal. I hate to see women cry." J.D. leaned back in the chair, his whole body sagging. "My mother cried when I left home. I hated that. And my sister cried when she came to visit me in the hospital after I took my bad spill at the rodeo. I hated that, too."

"I *said* I wasn't going to cry," Deanna snapped.

J.D. ignored her show of temper. "What we each ought to do is go shower. We haven't bathed since we started the charity drive."

"We don't have any clean clothes. They're all in the tack box."

J.D. shrugged. "This place has a laundry service. Just call room service and hang your clothes outside. They'll turn them around in no time."

"No."

"No?"

Deanna shook her head. "Not me. You can, though."

"For heaven's sake, why not?" J.D. was obviously exasperated. "We both smell like horses."

"My clothes smell like Rustler." Deanna blinked fast. "I'm not ready to wash him out of my life just yet."

"That's the silliest thing I ever—" J.D. broke off as a single lone tear rolled down Deanna's cheek. He swore, just once, and left his chair to join her on the bed.

"Damn it, Deanna." He pulled her head onto his shoulder and gently stroked her back. "You *promised*."

CHAPTER EIGHT

IN THE END Deanna did the sensible thing. At J.D.'s urging she headed for the shower and let him call for laundry service. Later, when they were both cleaned up, she even let him order dinner.

It was well after midnight when they sat down to eat, and she still wasn't hungry. But toying with her food—and being in J.D.'s company—was preferable to going to bed. She didn't think she could sleep. By the set of J.D.'s jaw, Deanna didn't think he would, either.

"Thanks for your help this afternoon," Deanna said, poking at her french fries. "I don't know what I would have done if you hadn't been there."

"I *wasn't* there," J.D. said with disgust. "I was in the men's room."

"It's not your fault," Deanna insisted. "Look at me. I was busy trying to reach my mother when it all happened. I wasn't much help, either."

"Did you ever get hold of her?"

"No, but I did leave a message on the answering machine. Mom will get it the next time she checks in. Then if Kathy phones Mom, she'll know what happened."

J.D. rose to his feet. "We should try to get some sleep. If we haven't heard anything by morning…"

Deanna hated hearing those words.

"I'll call my ranch and arrange for someone to pick us up."

Deanna stood up herself and walked with him to the door. J.D. paused at the threshold and softly touched her cheek. "Cheer up. They might find them yet."

Deanna wished with all her might that J.D. was right. "I had to hand-feed him, you know."

"Rustler?"

"Yes. He was so weak when I took him from the animal shelter that he couldn't eat. Even the IV wasn't enough, so I hand-fed him. It did the trick. I just hope that whoever has Rustler takes good care of him. And your gelding." She swallowed hard. "I suppose I owe you an apology. At least you were up front about wanting Rustler."

J.D. leaned one broad shoulder against the doorjamb, his expression inscrutable. "In other words, I'm a scoundrel, but I'm no horse thief?"

"Not a scoundrel, either." She impulsively gave him a quick kiss on the cheek. It was a gesture that surprised them both. "Thanks again, J.D. Sleep well."

"You, too," he said, but didn't move.

Deanna felt the air crackle with tension at his unspoken question. He wanted to stay; Deanna was certain of it. And she was sorely tempted to ask him to stay—more tempted than she'd ever been in her life—but what kind of a relationship could they have without complete trust? Deanna sighed and reached for the doorknob. Only then did J.D. leave, his face an unreadable mask in the hall's dim light.

Deanna pushed the door shut and leaned her head against it for a second. Then she reluctantly locked the dead bolt and kicked off her boots. Turning off the lights, she lay down on top of the bed fully clothed. As bad as she felt about Rustler's disappearance, sending J.D. away was worse.

He'd helped her so much today, especially at the police station. Rustler's disappearance had been traumatic, but

J.D.'s presence had made the situation easier. She closed her eyes, remembering how J.D. had held her close, his response to her tears a strange mixture of gentleness and exasperation. He was a good man to have around when times were bad.

She idly wondered what it would be like to have him around *all* the time. Maybe she should start considering that possibility. But her last thought before exhaustion overtook her was, *If only I could trust him....*

Deanna had only been asleep for a few hours when she was awakened by someone pounding on the door.

"Deanna? Let me in!"

"Huh?" She sat up, disoriented.

"It's J.D.!"

She turned on the lights and staggered toward the door. "What is it?" she asked as she let him in. "What's wrong?"

"They found my truck." He pushed past her and picked up her boots from the floor. "Here. Put these on. There's a squad car waiting for us outside."

"The horses?"

"They're all right," he said triumphantly. "Whoever stole them even watered and fed them."

"They didn't catch the thief?" Deanna asked as she shoved her feet into the boots.

"I'm afraid not." J.D. grabbed her arm and led her to the elevator. "But I'd rather have the horses than the thief."

Some of Deanna's joy over Rustler's being found faded. "You don't think the thief might come back for Rustler, do you? You yourself said he was valuable."

"No. This was no horse thief. Real horse thieves would have planned the crime better."

"I don't understand."

"Deanna, it was probably just a car thief who saw an opportunity and took it. Then panicked when things went wrong."

"Wrong?"

"Yes." J.D. smiled. "You know why the police were able to find my truck? Because it ran out of gas. The gas tank hadn't been filled before it was stolen, but the thief hadn't bothered to check. It was definitely amateur time. Believe me, I'd know a professional horse thief if I came across one."

Later, as they drove off to get the truck, the police officer confirmed J.D.'s words.

"I wouldn't worry about this happening again. It was probably some kid pulling a stupid prank. You and your boyfriend are lucky, though. Someone saw the truck abandoned on the side of the road with the horses still inside and called us."

"Are the horses really all right?"

"They weren't happy about being cooped up for so long, but they looked all right to me. Of course, I'm no vet."

"Well, I am, and I intend to see for myself. Can't you go any faster?"

J.D. grinned and took Deanna's hand. "You'll have to excuse my, er, girlfriend, officer. She's not a patient woman."

Deanna didn't argue with either statement. She could barely wait for the patrol car to stop once its headlights struck J.D.'s truck.

"Are the truck and trailer okay?" the officer asked J.D. as Deanna grabbed a flashlight from the tack box and entered the trailer's escape door, near the horses' heads.

"They seem fine," he replied, "except for the empty gas tank, of course."

"We put in a couple of gallons of gas. That should get you to the next service station. If you'll sign right here, I'll give you your keys. They were left in the ignition. No prints on them or elsewhere, I'm sorry to say. How are things inside the trailer?"

"Deanna?"

"The horses are okay," Deanna announced in relief. She'd been afraid that their standing in one position so long would have caused swollen tendons, but that wasn't the case.

"Thank goodness." J.D. helped her down from the trailer.

"I'm glad things turned out so well for you and the horses," said the policeman. "We'd best be on our way. Good night."

After they'd expressed their thanks, the squad car drove away, leaving Deanna and J.D. behind. Deanna breathed in the smell of the horses and sighed blissfully.

"Some night," J.D. remarked as he opened her truck door.

"You said a mouthful," Deanna replied as she hopped in. "I'm glad this nightmare's over," she added as he climbed into the truck. "I haven't had so much excitement since—" She broke off.

"Since when?" J.D. asked, starting the engine.

Since Mom's trial.

"For a long time." Deanna busied herself with her seat belt. "So, now what?"

"Gasoline first. And then we catch up with the wagon train, if you're still game."

"Oh, yes."

"I hope you won't lose much pledge money from the miles you missed. I'd like to make up the difference."

Deanna paused. This offer was yet one more thing that didn't fit the villainous image she'd had of him. Ever since the start of the charity drive, that old image had been falling away, piece by piece. She wasn't ready to trust him completely, but neither could she continue to condemn him. It was time she took another, closer look at J. D. Vaughn.

"That won't be necessary, J.D." Deanna gave his shoulder a grateful squeeze. "There are provisions for emergencies. Kathy can substitute for me. But thanks." J.D. had started to move toward her, but Deanna let her hand fall back in her lap. "Now let's get that gas."

They did, then they headed off to meet the wagon train. "We'll never find them in the dark," Deanna predicted. "If we drive on ahead to Maricopa Wells, they should catch up to us sometime before lunch. There are sleeping bags in your tack box, so we'll be able to get some sleep. The horses can stretch their legs and graze."

"Sounds good to me. Where does the trail go from Maricopa Wells?"

"We'll cross the Fortymile Desert and go through the Maricopa Mountains until we hit the Gila River. Then we follow the Gila west to the Colorado River—the state line. You might want to have your ranch pick up your truck and trailer and drive it ahead to Fort Yuma. That's where the trail ends."

"I'll stop at the next gas station and give them a call. In fact, I'll have them drop me off another horse before we leave."

"But... I checked your gelding. He's okay."

"Oh, I still plan to ride Pete. I just think Shawn might be a little tired of riding on the stage."

"Why would you say that? Shawn adores his mother."

"True, but Shawn's met a young lady his age who's riding her own horse. Tiffany's too bashful to ride on the stage with Kathy. Shawn seemed upset by the whole situation."

Deanna turned toward him in surprise. "I never would have pegged you for a romantic."

"That's because you aren't one yourself, so you don't notice it in other people," he said matter-of-factly, his eyes on the road.

"I'm not *that* blind. I notice you're still wearing my bandanna."

J.D.'s grin reminded her of the cat that ate the canary. "Ah, but am I wearing it because I'm being romantic? Or am I wearing it to remind you who has the whip hand?"

Deanna scowled. "Knowing you, it's probably the latter. And just because you bested me with staging trivia once doesn't mean you have the whip hand where *I'm* concerned."

"Doesn't it?"

"No!"

"Well, if I ever concede defeat, I'll return it to you. Until then—" he touched the blue triangle at his neck "—it's mine."

Deanna exhaled sharply. He'd been so nice to her when Rustler had disappeared. Now that the horses were safe, it seemed they were back where they'd started. Suddenly Deanna realized she was ready to include J.D. in her life. Maybe she would be his veterinarian.

Maybe something more...

Deanna's perceptions of him were changing. But she still didn't know which J.D. wanted more. Her or her horse? She was pondering that when J.D. began fiddling with his mirrors.

"You were right," he said. "Whoever stole my truck *was* shorter than I am."

Deanna wrapped her arms around herself. "It's creepy to think that whoever it was sat in this very seat."

J.D. said nothing, but he reached for her hand and held it tight.

"Don't you worry, Deanna. He won't get near this truck—or you—again. I guarantee it."

There was a dangerous edge to his voice that was frightening—yet very reassuring. It occurred to Deanna that she wouldn't want to be this man's enemy.

Just the opposite...

It was close to sunrise when they reached the Maricopa Wells area and stopped to eat. J.D. also managed to call his ranch to make arrangements for the extra horse.

After breakfast they were back on the road, heading for the part of Butterfield Trail that ran through the mountains. The Maricopas consisted mostly of creosote-covered flats, the pungent dark bushes growing among huge saguaros and lesser cacti. But at least there was water for the horses, and the air was cool.

J.D. and Deanna busied themselves tending the horses. J.D. gave them grain from the trailer's store, while Deanna set up the pickets. It was almost six when Deanna finally unrolled her sleeping bag.

"Not that you're going to need it," J.D. observed. "It feels like it's going to be another hot one."

"As long as it's peaceful, I can live with it." Deanna looked around. The sky was a brilliant turquoise, and a hawk circled high overhead, its sharp cry piercing the desert air.

She spread her bag in the shade of the horse trailer and lay down on top of it. She sighed blissfully and closed her eyes. After a couple of moments she asked, "Aren't you going to get some rest?"

"Nope."

Deanna opened her eyes. "Why not?" It was then that she saw him sitting on a camp stool with a gleaming rifle in his hands.

"*Where* did you get that?"

"I keep it locked up in my horse trailer."

Deanna sat up and stared at the walnut stock. "*What* are you doing with it?"

"I'm protecting my property."

"You're— J.D., don't be foolish!"

"What would you have me do, Deanna? Hand everything over on a silver platter?"

"Of course not! But no one's going to show up here in the middle of the desert! And even if they do, a truck isn't worth getting killed for! Even Rustler—as much as I care for him—isn't worth that!"

J.D. looked at her, his eyes as cold as the rifle's steel barrel. "No one takes what's mine, Deanna. I've lived by that rule since I was thirteen. I'm not going to change now."

Suddenly Deanna remembered the story about the grizzly who'd killed his horse. She remembered the awful scars on his body. She glanced from his face to the rifle, then back again. She'd never seen him look like that before.

"You said the thief was only an amateur. You said we'd never see him again."

"No. I said he wouldn't get near you again. And we've been followed. In fact, we're being watched right this minute."

"*What?* Where?" she said, frantically scanning the area around them.

"I spotted a rider over that rocky ridge to the west. I want you to go saddle my horse, Deanna."

"And just what are you going to do?" she asked suspiciously.

J.D.'s expression boded ill for that lone rider. "I'm going to check out the ridge."

She sprang to her feet. "Not without me, you're not!"

"Stay here, Deanna."

"And do what?"

"I want you to lock yourself in the truck while I go after a horse thief."

"Not on your life! It's not *your* horse they're after." Deanna defiantly got Rustler's saddle from the tack box.

"You'd be much safer," J.D. insisted, his eyes remaining fixed on the ridge.

"This isn't the Old West, for heaven's sake! I'm a modern woman. I don't take orders from some ex-rodeo cowboy. Besides," she added, "Maybe there's more than one. Maybe they want us to split up. Once you're gone, they could double back for Rustler."

The scowl on his face showed J.D. still didn't like the idea of her coming along.

"I'm serious!" she went on. "The Apaches used to wait at Pima Pass for the stagecoaches!"

"Where's the pass?"

"Between Maricopa Wells and the bend of the Gila River. It was a favorite ambush spot for the Apaches. If the thief gets Rustler and crosses the river, we'll never catch him."

"You mean me, not we, and I *will* catch him."

"I thought you were a liberated man. Remember, it was your sister who shot that bear. Would you tell her to get in the truck, lock the door and hide under the seat?"

"Hell, no."

"Well, you're not telling me to, either." She started saddling Rustler.

"All right, Deanna, you can come, but only if you do exactly as I say. I don't want you getting hurt."

"Neither do I."

Within minutes both horses were saddled and their riders mounted. J.D. slid his rifle into a scabbard on his saddle, and they were off, spurring their horses to a quick trot that would cover distance, yet not alarm their unwanted visitor or visitors.

"I wish we could see behind that ridge."

"We'll be able to in a minute," J.D. replied. "But there's no sense in alerting him by riding directly over. We'll stay on the trail, ride up to higher ground and get a look from there."

Deanna nodded. The area around them was rocky except for the faint dirt trail that was part of the original Butterfield Trail. It, along with stone remnants of the staging stations in the Maricopas, hadn't changed much in more than a century. Nor had the forbidding desolate landscape.

She nervously looked around for some trace of modern civilization, but all she saw was their truck and the deadly rifle in J.D.'s scabbard.

Modern woman though she was, Deanna was glad she wasn't alone in the middle of the desert, tracking horse thieves. After a moment she surveyed the terrain once more. It was comforting—very comforting—to have J.D. there.

"J.D., look!"

J.D.'s gaze followed the direction of her pointing finger. He saw a puff of dust that hung heavily in the still air of the desert.

"We *are* being followed!" she said.

"So it would seem. Deanna, stay here."

"Where are you going?"

J.D. gave her a look that sent shivers down her spine. "It's my turn to follow him."

"But—"

"Wait here." He turned off the trail and touched his heels to Pete's flanks. In an instant, the palomino was off at a quick canter.

She watched him ride off. Rustler pranced in place, seeming to sense Deanna's nervousness. When J.D. was close to cresting the ridge, Deanna saw a strange horse and rider make a swift descent. J.D. was caught going the wrong way as the stranger reached the trail in front of Deanna and took off.

In seconds Deanna made her decision. She let Rustler take the bit and gave chase.

The bay horse before her had a good head start, its speed hard to match. But Deanna didn't panic. She knew that the quarter horse would be unable to maintain that speed for long, and Rustler was still going faster. And faster...

Wind rushed through her hair, and she carefully maintained her balance as the rocks and hills and cacti melded into a blur. She held the saddlehorn with one hand, frightened yet exhilarated by the sheer power beneath her. The rider ahead gave Deanna a quick glance, and even from a distance Deanna could sense alarm in his movements.

She tucked her body lower and urged Rustler to even greater speed. The horse responded immediately, covering the ground in longer and longer strides until Deanna was breathless. All four of Rustler's feet became airborne again and again as he gained on the bay horse.

Deanna felt grim satisfaction at the other rider's dilemma. She and Rustler would run horse and rider ragged—even better, they'd run them into the ground. Rustler was invincible. And as long as Rustler was hers, so was she. From a distance she thought she heard her name being shouted, but it was blocked out by the pounding of the stallion's hooves, his snorting rhythmic breathing. She felt only the sheer joyous sensation of speed. She knew her horse was feeling the same primitive joy. This race was theirs—hers and Rustler's—and nothing could stop them.

Not even J.D., who was still calling her. The distance between the bay and the stallion was rapidly closing; the quarter horse visibly tiring. Deanna could see the heavy lather forming a white blanket on the brown flanks. On this straight dirt track there was no way Rustler could lose.

"We got them now, boy." Her hat flew off her head, only the chin strap keeping it around her neck. "They're ours."

And it seemed as if they were, until the bay abruptly left the trail and headed back onto the rocky desert terrain.

"No!" Deanna yelled as her prize eluded her. She struggled to slow Rustler's speed so she could follow. By the time she'd managed to control the excited stallion's forward momentum and turned him in the right direction, the bay had a big lead again.

And Rustler wasn't experienced with uneven ground. Deanna had always ridden him on bridle paths or in paddocks. But here, the quarter horse clearly had the advantage. He easily picked his way through the rocks and tall saguaros, zigging and zagging effortlessly with inbred agility. The thick muscular legs jumped narrow gullies effortlessly and scrambled down and up the sides of larger ones, if not with grace and style, then with efficiency and determination.

Deanna's heart sank. Rustler was no quarter horse. She guided him around the obstacles, but she had to do it carefully. Despite his attempts to please, Rustler's slender legs were bred for running, not scrambling. Deanna could have screamed with frustration as she saw the bay pull farther and farther away. She didn't have a chance of catching him, or the thief.

But J.D. did. She heard the palomino's hoofbeats behind her and turned in the saddle.

J.D. was avoiding the cactus and boulders, his knees only whispers away from the obstacles, like a champion barrel racer. He took the S-shaped turns tight and fast, moving with the same agility as the bay. But with, Deanna saw with delight, greater speed.

"Stay put!" J.D. ordered as he passed her. "I'll take it from here!"

"Not on your life," she yelled. She followed J.D., not at the same breakneck pace, but as quickly and safely as she could. Her blood pounded with excitement as J.D. got closer and closer—until the bay was only a few lengths ahead of the palomino.

"Get 'em, J.D.!" she screamed fiercely. "They can't last much longer!"

She saw first the bay then the palomino scramble down and out of a dried flood wash, the dusty gravel bed churning under the eight powerful legs. At Deanna's urging, Rustler continued toward them. J.D. was inches away from catching their thief, and she wanted to be there when he did.

She and Rustler reached the edge of the wash. His delicate ears pricked forward as he hesitated.

"It's okay, boy. Just take it slow, and we'll be fine."

Rustler saw the palomino in the distance. The instinct to rejoin his trail companion was strong, so he started forward. Unfortunately his experience descending washes was nonexistent. Instead of sliding down the bank on his rump, he gathered his long legs under him for a jump.

"Rustler, no!" Deanna cried. She pulled back on the reins, but it was too late.

Rustler launched himself toward the bottom of the creek bed. But the wash was too deep and wide, and Rustler's landing fell short. Deanna felt his hooves scramble for purchase in the unstable gravel of the bank, felt his muscles tremble, felt him list heavily to the side.

She screamed—more out of fear for Rustler's graceful legs snapping than fear for herself—and tried to compensate by shifting her balance to aid his.

It was no use. Rustler was strong, but he was no match for gravity. With a neigh of terror that mingled with J.D.'s frantic "Deanna!" Rustler fell, his rider still in the saddle.

Deanna lay motionless, her face in the dirt, both feet in the stirrups. Rustler had landed on his side, his massive body, not his legs taking the blow. Totally winded, she could feel his heartbeat against one leg, but heard no frantic breathing. She made no move to get up, for she was trapped under Rustler.

After a few agonizing seconds the air rushed back into both their lungs, and she moaned. Lord, what a mess she'd made of things!

"Deanna! Deanna!"

Still astride Pete, J.D. was coming down the side of the wash. The dust and gravel churned up by the palomino's hooves stung her face, forcing her to close her eyes.

"Oh, my God," she heard him say. Then she heard him dismount and rush to her side. "Open your eyes," he ordered as he knelt by her head, his hands on her cheeks. "Damn you, open them!"

Deanna did—mostly out of surprise. Even during their worst arguments, he'd never sworn at her. Stranger still, his face was white beneath his tan. Deanna blinked at the sight, then coughed from the dirt.

"You little idiot! Where are you hurt?" he asked roughly, although the hands brushing the debris from her hair and face were gentle.

"I don't think I am," she said, still amazed by the look of shock on his face.

"Any numbness? Tingling? Pain in your back or neck?"

"Not a thing. As falls go, this wasn't bad at all."

J.D. spat out a vicious expletive that made Deanna flinch. "I saw the whole thing. Don't tell me it wasn't bad!"

There was nothing Deanna could say to that. Frankly, she was too glad to see him to argue.

"How's Rustler? Will you get him up? His legs should be okay."

J.D. didn't answer. His face was almost unrecognizable as he eased her right leg out of the stirrup and boot, then ran his hands up and down it.

"J.D.? What about Rustler?" Deanna repeated. "Aren't you going to check him out?"

"Let's get you taken care of, then you can see to the horse."

"Well, that makes sense— I'm the vet, after all."

"I can probably get him up, but you'll have to kick your trapped foot out of the stirrup first." He reached for Rustler's reins. "Do you..." J.D.'s voice broke as he studied the huge trembling horse lying on top of her. "Do you think you can move it?"

With every ounce of strength she had, Deanna managed to flex her trapped foot. Rustler shifted slightly at the movement, but J.D. held him still.

"I don't think it's broken. The sand here is pretty soft.... There!" she said with satisfaction as she moved it another few inches. "It's out of the stirrup."

J.D. nodded, a bit of color coming back into his face for the first time. "All right. I'm going to pull Rustler's head. That should do the trick. But I want you to stay still."

"I'm fine," Deanna insisted.

"Don't argue!" The words cracked like a whip, and Deanna stared at him. Who was this stranger? Where was the calm man who always seemed to have everything under control?

"I'll keep his hooves away from you, so don't move. Ready? Here goes."

J.D. clicked his tongue and pulled on the reins. Rustler raised his head and with very little urging began to scramble to his feet. Deanna slid her free leg over the saddle and breathed a sigh of relief as she and Rustler were finally separated. That sigh turned into a gasp as the blood rushed back into her numb foot, causing a shooting pain.

"Deanna?" J.D. threw Rustler's reins to the ground and was back at her side in an instant, gently removing her other boot and feeling for injuries.

"It's okay. Just a little numb." Suddenly she remembered the thief and sat up straight.

"I told you to stay still!" he yelled. "You might have a spinal injury!" He tried to press her back down onto the sand, but Deanna wouldn't cooperate.

"J.D., where is he?"

He stared at her in disbelief, his hands still on her shoulders. "Who?"

"The thief. What did you do with him? Did you tie him up?"

He shook his head, and a terrible suspicion crept into Deanna's mind. She shook off his hands, grabbed for her boots and yanked them onto her feet.

"You let him get away? Rustler and I wore him out for you, and you let him get away?" She was almost shrieking. "How *could* you?"

"I thought you were hurt! What did you expect me to do?"

"Catch the thief, tie him up, *then* come back for me," Deanna said promptly. "I wasn't hurt, and neither was Rustler. We were just winded."

To Deanna's confusion, J.D. looked as if he wanted to throttle her. "How the hell was I supposed to know that? You had no business running your horse over strange terrain!"

"The thief had no business trying to steal Rustler, and he deserves to go to jail. We almost had him!"

"Only because you nearly got yourself killed!" J.D. ran his fingers through his hair. "Which makes no more sense than your chasing my stolen truck in Tucson! For a woman with a fancy education, you sure aren't strong in the brains department!"

"You were chasing him, too!" Deanna retorted angrily. "Besides, it's my horse he wants, not yours. No one fights my battles while I sit on the sidelines."

"That's exactly where you belong! I knew what I was doing! While you—" he pointed a finger in her face and glared at her "—you could have died!"

"I didn't!" Deanna pushed his finger away, anger over J.D.'s attitude mixing with disappointment. "And even if I'd broken my neck, at least we could have put the scum behind bars!"

Immediately she knew she'd gone too far. J.D.'s eyes filled with some terrible violent emotion.

"Thief or no thief, no desert wash is going to break your lovely neck, lady. That's a privilege I reserve for myself." Then he jerked her hard into his arms.

Deanna gasped against his mouth. His kiss was brutal, punishing and primitive—as primitive and exciting as her wild ride on Rustler. She didn't flinch from his assault. Instead, she replied with one of her own, giving into her own fierce emotions.

Here was a man as strong-willed as she, as determined as she, as immovable as she. The two of them were locked in battle, and Deanna reveled in every minute of it. She'd be damned if she'd retreat.

CHAPTER NINE

"DEANNA, I CAN'T BELIEVE you actually ran after the thieves who stole J.D.'s truck!" Kathy gasped.

It was night and the four of them, Kathy, Shawn, J.D. and Deanna were seated around a small camp fire. Deanna had spent an exhausting day answering questions from everyone in the wagon train, along with reporters who'd heard of the abduction and shown up to cover the story. She and J.D. hadn't had a minute to themselves, much to her disgust.

"Thief. We only saw one."

"But you could have been killed! What a crazy thing to do!"

"Kathy, you don't know the half of it," J.D. muttered. Deanna ignored him, for although she'd told Kathy about the theft of the truck, she'd given only scant details about the wild ride in the desert and her fall. She had enough aches and bruises—not to mention dark looks from J.D.— to remind her of what had happened, and she simply didn't want to talk about it anymore. Thinking about it—especially his kiss—was something else. Unfortunately that kiss seemed to be the furthest thing from his mind.

J.D. had been furious with her. He'd given her the worst tongue-lashing she'd ever received in her life soon after he'd gotten both her and Rustler to their feet. The whole time she'd been examining Rustler, he'd yelled at her for coaxing the stallion to take the wash and called her an idiot at least a dozen times for moving when he'd told her to stay still. That wasn't the end of it, either.

When J.D.'s men had eventually arrived to pick up J.D.'s truck and trailer, as well as leave the spare horse for Shawn, Deanna and J.D. had argued further. J.D. had wanted to drive her to the nearest hospital. Deanna had emphatically refused. For one thing, she was afraid to leave Rustler. More importantly, she didn't want to prematurely end the little time she had remaining with J.D.

She'd finally convinced him to let her remount the un-injured Rustler and rejoin the wagon train. Even then J.D. had insisted she be looked at by the wagon train's nurse. When she thought about it, J.D.'s reaction to her fall seemed out of proportion. After all, he'd been a rodeo rider. He knew that most falls looked much worse than they actually were. And as if that wasn't bewildering enough, J.D. hadn't even looked at Rustler until *after* the nurse pronounced Deanna fit.

Deanna's feelings toward J.D. were muddled. The more she was with the man, the more she wanted to be with him. She needed time to think over everything—to try to make sense of the emotions she'd felt while in his arms. But all anyone wanted to do was talk about what had happened in Tucson.

"One reporter told me," Kathy said, "his headline was going to read, 'Horse thieves threaten charity drive.' He said it would be good publicity, but I don't think my sponsors will be pleased to read it."

Deanna groaned, more because Kathy wouldn't drop the subject than because of any headlines.

Shawn's wide eyes reflected the flickering fire. "Your patients will be talking about it for weeks." Deanna frowned. She hadn't even considered that aspect. "Gee, Dr. Leighton, do you think the thieves will come back?"

"Shawn! Don't even say that!" Kathy said sharply. "That's the last thing we need."

"Actually what we need is some sleep." J.D. rose to his feet. "Deanna and I were up most of last night. I'm going to check on the horses, then go to bed."

"Me, too," Deanna replied.

"I'm going to bed down by the main camp fire," Kathy announced as she stood up. "There's lots of people around. It should be good and safe. Why don't you come too, Deanna?"

"No, thanks. It's too noisy. Besides, I want to be near Rustler. I'm staying here."

"I don't know if Shawn and I should leave you alone."

J.D. put his hand on Deanna's shoulder. "She won't be, Kathy. You two go ahead. I'm sure your friends will be glad to see you, Shawn."

"Anyone in particular?" Kathy asked, maternal curiosity apparently overriding any desire she might have had to comment on J.D.'s caress of Deanna's shoulder. "Like maybe that girl you were talking to today? Tiffany, isn't it? That was nice of J.D. to bring you a mount so you two could ride together."

"Aw, Mom." Shawn sounded so uncomfortable that Deanna had to fight to keep a straight face.

"I guess Kathy's finally come up against some competition," said J.D. as mother and son walked toward the center of the wagon circle.

"She won't mind." Deanna accepted J.D.'s proffered hand as she painfully started to get up. "I suppose I should move Rustler closer to the stagecoach."

"I already did," J.D. assured her. "Pete, too. And I'll be sleeping outside the wagon circle tonight."

Deanna nodded. "Good idea. Between the two of us, we should be able to keep an eye on Rustler."

"No. Kathy's right. You should sleep by the main fire."

"Why? Do you think guard duty is too dangerous for the weaker sex?"

"For women in general? No. For a woman who's been through what you have, yes. Take my word for it, you'll be stiff and sore in the morning."

She was stiff and sore now, but she'd die rather than admit it.

"You're in no shape to defend yourself, let alone Rustler."

"I'm in fine shape."

"You're limping."

"I am not!"

"Liar."

Deanna glared at him. "There's a difference between limping and favoring."

"Well, you'll *favor* that leg next to the camp fire, not next to Rustler."

Deanna tossed her head and placed her sleeping bag exactly where she wanted it. But J.D. had the last word on the subject. He even enlisted Kathy's aid by seeking her out and deliberately telling her about Deanna's tumble. After more unwanted attention and fussing, Deanna was forced to capitulate. In a foul temper, she retired to her sleeping bag, which was now spread next to Kathy's inside the wagon circle. J.D. and Shawn settled down near the horses, planning to take turns guarding them.

The night dragged by. An hour passed, then another and another, and still Deanna couldn't sleep. Finally she gave up trying. She was wide awake thinking about J.D. and feeling anxious about Rustler. Grabbing her flashlight, she went to check on the horses. J.D. awoke as she approached his sleeping bag.

He held his hand up in front of his eyes to block the flashlight's glare. "Deanna?"

"Yes."

He rose on one elbow. "Would you please get that light out of my face? It's bright enough to stop a train."

Deanna obliged, focusing on his bare chest, instead.

"Why aren't you sleeping?" he asked with a yawn.

"I was worried about the horses." She didn't add that thoughts of him had greatly contributed to her insomnia.

"Go back to bed. Everything's under control," J.D. said in a voice hoarse with sleep.

"Is it?" Deanna deliberately shone her flashlight toward Shawn's empty sleeping bag. "With you sleeping and Shawn missing, I wouldn't say so."

J.D. reacted instantly. With a curse he unzipped his sleeping bag. "Toss me my jeans," he ordered tersely. "Then look and see if that little mare I brought for Shawn is still tethered next to Kathy's team."

Deanna gave him the jeans that were draped over his saddle, then turned her flashlight on the nearby team. They were picketed close to Rustler and Pete; she could count all six of them. But the little strawberry roan J.D. had loaned Shawn was gone.

"The mare's missing," Deanna reported to J.D., who was pulling on his boots

J.D. swore again.

"Where in the world would Shawn go on horseback this late at night?" she asked.

He raised an eyebrow. "Boy meets girl, boy wants to be alone with girl."

"Not Shawn! He'd never . . . I mean, he's not that kind of boy!"

"He's fifteen years old," J.D. said harshly. "That's old enough to know better."

"Shawn's a good kid!" Deanna insisted. "Whatever he and Tiffany have planned, I'm certain it's harmless enough. A few kisses and cuddles, at most."

"That's not what I'm talking about. Shawn promised to take the first watch so I could sleep. He lied to me." J.D. stood up and reached for his shirt. "He's not going to get away with it, either."

"J.D.! You aren't going to go breaking in on them, are you? Shawn will be so embarrassed!"

"He's going to feel more than just embarrassed by the time I'm through with him," J.D. promised grimly. "And to think I let him borrow one of my horses!"

"There's nothing wrong with a healthy attraction between boys and girls," Deanna said uneasily, not liking the expression on J.D.'s face. Shawn was in serious trouble. And maybe so was Tiffany.

"There's nothing wrong with a little responsibility, either. Shawn promised to stand guard, not ride off into the night without telling anyone where he was going. What if he or Tiffany got hurt?"

Deanna's eyes widened at the thought.

"Exactly. Shawn should know better," he repeated. "They both should."

Deanna couldn't deny that. "What are you going to do?"

"What do you think?" J.D. snapped as he searched for his flashlight. "I'm going to find them. I have a pretty good idea where they might be."

"Where?"

"We passed a small cave before we settled down for the night. If I was looking for a secluded spot, that's where I'd go."

"I'll go tell Kathy and saddle Rustler."

"No, you stay here," J.D. ordered in a tone that brooked no argument. "This is between Shawn and me. No one else."

Deanna watched as he saddled the palomino and rode off. She turned her attention to Rustler. His ears had pricked up at the departure of the palomino, and his proud head swung toward Deanna.

"Sorry, boy. We weren't invited along." Deanna patted the stallion's neck, then sighed. "It's back to bed for us."

Deanna sat down cross-legged on top of J.D.'s sleeping bag, desperately wishing she was with him. There was no sense going back to her own sleeping bag. Someone had to watch Rustler. It might as well be her.

"Deanna? Deanna!"

Deanna heard Kathy's frantic voice. "I'm right here, Kathy."

Kathy came rushing out from behind the Concord stage. "Deanna, is Tiffany with you? I woke up, and she was—" Kathy abruptly broke off. "Where are Shawn and J.D.?"

Deanna took no pleasure in answering that question, or in Kathy's reaction.

"I can't believe Shawn would sneak off without telling anyone where he was going!" Kathy gasped. "He knows how dangerous that is!"

"J.D. will find them," Deanna assured her. "In the meantime, he wants us to sit calmly and wait."

But calmness proved to be impossible. Less than fifteen minutes later Shawn recklessly came galloping back on J.D.'s little mare. Deanna was horrified by the blood on Shawn's face, by his news.

There had been a small rock slide at the cave—a common occurrence among the dry brittle rocks in the desert—and Tiffany had been hurt.

"She can't ride," Shawn sobbed. "Mr. Vaughn wants the nurse and the medical wagon out there. I'm going back."

"You're hurt yourself!" Kathy said, grabbing the horse's reins to stop her son from wildly taking off again. "You stay with me. You're in no shape to be riding."

"I have to help Tiffany!" Shawn exclaimed frantically, but Kathy was firm.

"Get off the horse, Shawn. You're not going anywhere."

"Your mother's right," Deanna said. "I'll take the nurse to Tiffany. She's at that little cave a couple of miles back, right?"

Shawn hesitated, nodded and finally dismounted. Deanna took the mare's reins in one hand, before examining Shawn's head laceration. She shook her head in dismay.

"You're going to need stitches. That's a nasty cut. Kathy, you take Shawn to the nurse and get him taken care of. I'll take the first-aid kit out to J.D. and see what I can do."

"Tiffany needs the nurse more than I do!" Shawn insisted.

"Shawn, you've had a head injury. I think it should be looked at before the nurse leaves."

"I'm fine!"

"You're not," Kathy said.

"You don't know that. You're no doctor, Mom!" Shawn protested as Kathy pressed a bandanna to Shawn's bleeding forehead. "And neither is she!"

"I may not be a people doctor, but I've set my share of broken bones and seen my share of cuts," Deanna said, mounting Shawn's mare. "I'll go get that first-aid kit. Kathy, have Tiffany's parents ride out with the nurse."

Shawn protested again, but Deanna ignored him. She hurried to the nurse's wagon, then she was off. Between the full moon and her flashlight she was easily able to see the trail and make good progress to the cave.

The first thing she noticed when she got there was all the fallen rubble and rocks lying at the entrance. The sound of the mare's hooves brought J.D. outside immediately, waving his hand to show her where he was and take her to Tiffany.

"How is she?" J.D. asked moments later. Tiffany's face was streaked with tears, but despite her pain she bravely submitted to Deanna's examination. In between sobs Tiffany told them about the rock slide and how Shawn had pushed her out of the way.

"That must have been some push," Deanna said, her fingers probing carefully. "Your shoulder's dislocated."

"I did that when I fell. Shawn got me away from the rocks. They fell on him, not me. How is he? I know he was hurt!" she cried. "His head was bleeding!"

"A few stitches and he'll be fine," Deanna said briskly. "And so will you be, once I fix your shoulder."

"Can you?"

"Sure. I've done this dozens of times." Deanna didn't tell her that the dislocations had been on animals, not humans, but the principle was the same. "J.D., take her in your lap and hold her still. Tiffany, try to relax. I'll have to pull hard on your arm to get the angle right. It'll hurt, but once it's back in the socket, most of the pain will disappear. Ready?"

Tiffany nodded, and Deanna reached for the girl's arm.

"Okay. Close your eyes, take a deep breath and count to three out loud."

As soon as Tiffany closed her eyes, Deanna mouthed to J.D., "On two." He nodded in understanding and tightened his hold on Tiffany.

Tiffany breathed deeply and slowly exhaled. "One..."

Deanna gently lifted the arm and brought it into position. Tiffany gasped, but managed to say, "Two..."

Deanna lifted higher and pulled at the same time. Over Tiffany's scream was the audible sound of bone clicking back into place. Tiffany slumped in J.D.'s arms, and he shifted his hold on her, careful not to jar her shoulder.

"Poor kid. She's fainted," J.D. said, stroking her forehead.

"I hated hurting her. Thank goodness I fixed it first try."

"You do good work, Doc." Approval showed on J.D.'s face.

Deanna grinned. "Not bad for a vet." She removed a sling from the first-aid kit. "At least she won't be in so much pain when she comes to."

"How's Shawn?" J.D. asked as Deanna worked to immobilize Tiffany's arm.

"Last I heard, the nurse was stitching up his head. I think it was more of a glancing blow than a direct hit. He's lucky. From the look of these rocks, Shawn could have taken one heck of a wallop. As it is, he'll probably have a headache for a few days."

J.D. muttered a few harsh words about Shawn's behavior. Deanna couldn't condone his language, but she certainly agreed with the sentiment.

"Tiffany's parents will be here with the wagon as soon as the nurse finishes with Shawn. I don't think either one will need a hospital tonight."

"Thank heavens for that."

Deanna looked at him sharply. "The way you took after these two, I wondered if you weren't ready to put Shawn in the hospital yourself."

"I wanted to shake some sense into him. Can you blame me?" J.D. gestured toward Tiffany's motionless body. "What happened here just proves my point."

"Well, I'd say the two of them have learned their lesson. Especially Shawn. He was bound and determined to come back here for Tiffany. Kathy practically had to drag him off his horse to have his head checked." Deanna tidied the first-aid kit, then closed it. "I wouldn't be surprised if he shows up with the nurse."

Deanna's prediction was correct. When the nurse and wagon arrived a short time later, Shawn was indeed there, along with Tiffany's parents and Kathy. The next few minutes were chaotic, with tears from the revived Tiffany as she was loaded into the wagon, profuse apologies from Shawn and comforting words from the parents.

Finally, however, the wagon left. Tiffany would go home in the morning. With the nurse's consent, Shawn would finish out the ride, although the nurse insisted he sit on the stagecoach, instead of J.D.'s mare.

Deanna and J.D. followed on the horses.

"I'm so glad those two are going to be okay," Deanna said softly. "I can't believe Shawn was so foolish."

J.D. turned sharply in his saddle, his eyes on hers. "This from the woman who nearly killed herself in a desert wash? Not to mention risking potential injury to her horse."

"I knew what I was doing," Deanna said tartly. "And I thought we were finished with that subject. I've had enough stress for one night without you dragging Rustler into this."

J.D. paused, then asked, "Why didn't you ride him out here?"

"Rustler wasn't saddled, but the mare was. I was in a hurry to see how Tiffany was, so I took her. I know I should have asked your permission, but—" She broke off at the look on his face, a look that bothered her. "What?"

His next question was delivered so casually that it made her suspicious.

"I don't suppose you asked anyone to keep an eye on Rustler while you were gone?"

Deanna bit her lip. "No. What with all the confusion, I didn't even think of doing that." A sudden dread filled her. "J.D., you don't think..."

She couldn't bring herself to finish.

"I think we should check on him," J.D. said firmly.

J.D. touched his heels to Pete's side, allowing the palomino to cautiously canter through the darkness and overtake the wagon. Deanna wasn't far behind. The ride back to the wagons seemed to take forever, but as soon as the circle became visible Deanna sought out the stallion's familiar form.

Even before J.D. clenched his reins in anger, even before her heart had a chance to accept what her eyes told her was true, Deanna knew.

Rustler was gone.

"YOU'RE NOT GOING after him, Shawn," Deanna said. "Not with that lump on your head."

"I'm fine, and I'm going!" Shawn declared.

It was morning. Deanna and J.D. had spent a good hour the night before searching the immediate area on horseback. Rustler's picket pin was still firmly in the ground, the line intact. Someone had released him at the halter end. But nothing more could be found in the dark, so the search had been put off.

"No, Shawn," J.D. said. He was saddling the mare for Deanna. Pistol Pete was already saddled and waiting. "Deanna's using the mare now."

"I could use Tiffany's horse. Her parents won't be leaving for another hour."

"No. The nurse said you could only ride on the stage. She said no horseback riding until your head stops hurting," Kathy reminded him.

"It's my fault Rustler's missing! If I'd been watching him, instead of sneaking off..." Shawn swallowed hard. "I want to come along."

"You'll stay with your mother," J.D. ordered. "Or can't you follow directions about *this,* either?"

Shawn paled, and Deanna's heart went out to him. Still, J.D. was right. Shawn needed to stay near the nurse and the wagon train. Even without the lump on his head, he was too upset over Tiffany to be of much use. As it was, Deanna's own stomach was a sick bundle of nerves.

The wagon master joined them.

"I've radioed the police in Phoenix for you," he told them with a look on his face that plainly added, *For all the good it will do.*

"Thanks," Deanna forced herself to say. "I'm sure they'll get in touch with the Tucson police."

"I guess it was your horse the thief in Tucson wanted, after all," the man concluded. "Not Mr. Vaughn's truck."

"I'm afraid so." Deanna kicked angrily at the dirt.

"The confusion sure made it easy for those thieves. What happened in Tucson must have been planned in advance." The wagon master shook his head in dismay. "This has been the wildest wagon train I've ever led."

Deanna couldn't argue with that.

"Are you ready to go?" J.D. asked.

"Yes. Kathy, you have my pledge papers?"

"I sure do. Shawn can log your miles for you so your sponsors don't feel cheated."

"Thanks, Shawn."

"You two be careful," Kathy said. "Good luck." And then she was waving goodbye. J.D. and Deanna mounted their horses and headed out.

"The wagon master said there's paved road about twenty miles southeast. Anyone stealing a horse would have to leave the area from there," J.D. said once they'd left the wagon train behind.

"What good will finding the road do?" Deanna sighed. "We aren't going to find Rustler there."

"No, but we might find a clue as to the identity of the thief."

"Like what? Tire tracks? Maybe a dropped wallet? J.D., this isn't the movies. We aren't going to find a thing," Deanna said dispiritedly. "Why don't you admit we're just going through the motions?"

"We might find something."

"And if we don't then what? Do we catch up to the wagon train?"

"No. I gave the wagon master my ranch number. He'll radio a messenger service at the next town for me. They'll contact my ranch and have my men meet us near the road with a truck and trailer."

"Why can't we go on ahead to the next town? It's not that far."

"Because I wanted to backtrack and see what we could find," he explained patiently. "And because after we talk, I don't think you'll want to go back to the wagon train."

Deanna gave him a sharp look. "Are you going to tell me why?"

"Yes, now that we're alone."

Deanna gazed at the emptiness of the desert surrounding them. "Well, we're certainly that. Go ahead."

J.D. reined his gelding in closer to the mare. "I've been thinking about the thief, Deanna—about who would profit by stealing your horse."

"Any Thoroughbred breeder, according to you," Deanna said with exasperation.

"No. Even if they knew about his bloodlines, Rustler doesn't have a racing record that would tempt a breeder to steal him. The reason I'm interested is that I own Rustler's dam. No, I think whoever took Rustler is someone local— someone who knows both you and the horse."

"I can't think of anyone who would do such a thing."

"But I have to be right," J.D. maintained. "It has to be someone who knew about the charity drive. Someone who was familiar with the route and the schedule."

Deanna shook her head. "You're grasping at straws. The whole town of Cactus Gulch knew where I was going the day I left, and they knew I was riding Rustler. Anyone could have followed me. Most of them are able horse-men."

"Did you tell anyone Rustler was papered?"

"I didn't have to. It was common knowledge at the humane society. Anyone local could have found out about Rustler from them."

J.D. frowned. "That doesn't narrow things down much, and it certainly won't help us recover Rustler. Papers can be altered or forged if they sell him."

"Rustler does have a lip tattoo," Deanna reminded him. "It would identify him."

"Tattoos can be altered, too. And if he was shipped to a foreign racing stable—say in South America—they wouldn't even bother to do that."

"But surely no one would pay all that money to get him out of the country? He's not *that* valuable, is he?"

"With all four legs sound? Deanna, trust me, he is."

Deanna didn't like the sound of that. If he was valuable enough to be shipped overseas, anyone, even J.D. himself, could be responsible for Rustler's theft.

"Maybe his original owner found out how good he was and stole him back." J.D. pushed his hat off his forehead. "We should check there."

"I already have. I've had the SPCA watching him ever since I acquired Rustler and had him prosecuted. I talked to them from the hotel in Tucson, and they don't think he was involved. The man knew what he had and simply lost interest. As far as he's concerned, Rustler was just a bad investment, especially after I reported him to the SPCA."

"I understand he was fined."

"The courts should have done more than that. Ironic isn't it? The man beat and starved the horse, but got off with a fine, while innocent people like my mother—" She broke off. What was it about J.D. that always had her blurting things out?

"What?" J.D. asked.

"Nothing."

"Deanna, you can talk to me. I won't betray a trust."

"I told you it was nothing." Deanna tried to change the subject back to Rustler. "Anyway, I don't think that guy is interested in Rustler now."

For the next few miles, she and J.D. rode in silence. The day grew longer, and the heat of the desert increased. After a while a rocky outcropping appeared, providing a rare patch of shade. They stopped under it and dismounted, then drank from their canteens, gratefully stretching their legs after so long in the saddle. Eventually J.D. removed Deanna's bandanna from around his neck, wet it and passed it to her.

"Thanks." She sponged her face, then handed it back. Already the damp cloth was warm with the heat. Funny how he'd never made any effort to return it to her. The cheap cotton bandanna was certainly at odds with his expensive silk shirts.

J.D. wiped his own face. "Days like this make me wish I was back at the Rocking J. First thing I did when I bought it was plant lots of shade trees."

"It sounds heavenly. I wish our landlord would plant some. You can grow just about anything in Arizona, if you can afford to irrigate, that is. We had this huge garden at our old place, before we moved to Cactus Gulch. Water is expensive in the desert, but Mom wasn't stingy when it came to the garden." Deanna smiled. "She grew the biggest tomatoes you ever saw."

J.D. hung his canteen back on the saddle, then said, "Tell me about your mother."

Deanna was instantly on her guard. "Well, she's a good woman. Sad since my father died, of course, but then his death was so tragic."

"She seems terribly devoted to you."

"Maybe too much. I keep hoping she'll find someone to replace Dad, but she's afraid to leave me alone at the clinic." Deanna shrugged. "Silly, really. I'm young and strong. I could handle it all if I had to. In fact, I'd be pleased if Mom wanted to do something else. She deserves better."

Deanna replaced her canteen, then swept a patch of ground clean with her boot and sat down. J.D. watched her settle herself more comfortably before joining her.

"I imagine your mother feels that way about you."

"Me? I'll never leave Cactus Gulch. At least, not for a long, long time."

"Unless your mother forces you to go. Unless she feels *you* deserve better."

Something in his voice made the hairs of the back of Deanna's neck stand on end. "What are you saying, J.D.?"

Immediately his face was shuttered.

"J.D.? Answer me!"

J.D. answered, but his words gave nothing away. "Your mother loves you very much, Deanna. When a person loves someone a great deal, sometimes they do desperate things. Try to remember that."

He helped a confused Deanna to her feet and refused to say anything further as they remounted and rode on. A short while later a hot desert wind started to blow. And with it went any trace of tracks. Deanna fought back the tears. She'd never expected to find anything, but realized she'd been hoping they would just the same.

Riding was slow, but fortunately the wind was at their backs. Eventually they reached a paved road. The wagon master had apparently radioed ahead to J.D.'s ranch, for after they'd been on the road for a short time, J.D.'s truck became visible. Deanna swallowed a lump in her throat as she watched the mare take the place in the horse trailer that Rustler had occupied. Pete was then loaded, and the hired men climbed into the trailer with the horses, leaving the truck for Deanna and J.D.

"Come on, Deanna. I'm taking you home."

J.D. offered her his hand on the drive, but although she accepted his comfort, she couldn't trust him. J. D. Vaughn had always wanted one thing from her—Rustler. Now Rustler was gone, and despite her feelings toward J.D., she had to be honest with herself. Rustler could very well be headed for South America with some of J.D.'s ranch hands. His solicitous concern could very well be a ploy designed to make her believe he was innocent.

If only she didn't always have to be the strong one—the one who took care of her mother and the debts and the practice. If only she could lean on someone once in a while. *If only J. D. Vaughn could be that someone.*

J.D. released Deanna's hand when he stopped to use a pay phone.

"I want one of my men to meet us with my car. It's too hot for the horses to travel all the way to your place, then back to mine."

Deanna nodded. She was silent until an hour later when the vehicle exchange had been made. She fastened her seat belt in J.D.'s fancy car, the one he'd first driven into Cactus Gulch.

"So tell me," she said bravely once they were under way. "Do you think I'll ever see Rustler again?"

To her surprise, J.D. kept his gaze on the road—almost as if he was afraid to look at her.

"I'm not a child. You can be honest."

J.D. did glance at her then. "I think we'll find your horse. In fact, I think I know who took him."

Deanna's eyes widened in shock. Surely he wasn't going to admit his guilt now? And possibly try to make amends? Could she forgive him if he did? "Who? Tell me!"

"Not until I'm certain."

Deanna's hopes for both the return of Rustler and a future with J.D. disappeared.

As if able to read her mind, J.D. said, "You'll get him back, Deanna."

She sighed heavily. "You needn't throw me a bone, J.D. I'm trying to be realistic."

J.D. made no response, prompting Deanna to say, "For someone who claims to know where Rustler is, you don't sound too happy about it."

"Theft isn't a laughing matter," was his last comment on the subject.

"We're almost home," Deanna said with surprise. Her mind had been so preoccupied she'd barely noticed the passage of time. "This is our turn. J.D., please hurry. My mother must be worried sick."

J.D. complied silently. Finally they were outside the house. Deanna grabbed for the door handle, anxious to see her mother, but hesitated when J.D. put a strong hand on her arm.

"What's the matter?"

"Wait. I want us to go in together."

"Oh. Okay." Deanna stared at him, concerned by the tight set of his jaw. "Are you all right?"

"I've been better." He went around and opened her door, then helped her out. "Come on, let's get this over with."

J.D. walked her up the stairs to their apartment. Helen hurried to meet them on the porch.

"Deanna!" Helen embraced her daughter. "I'm glad you're home."

"I'm glad to *be* home." Deanna returned the hug, then drew away, her face sad. "I guess you've heard about Rustler."

"Honey, I'm so sorry. I know how much he meant to you, but there will be other horses some d—"

"Mrs. Leighton, your daughter's getting Rustler back."

"Back?"

"Yes. I know who took him."

To Deanna's horror, her mother's face turned pale. For a moment, she thought Helen was going to faint. She grabbed her mother and lowered her onto the porch swing.

"Mom, what's wrong? Do you want a glass of water?"

Helen didn't answer as Deanna patted her mother's shoulder and rubbed her arm. "Have you been working too hard? I told you not to overdo things while I was gone."

Helen hid her face in her hands. Even then, Deanna didn't understand what was wrong until J.D. said, "Do you want to tell her, Mrs. Leighton, or shall I?"

Deanna slowly straightened, her hand falling away from her mother's arm. "Tell me what?"

J.D. drew a long breath. "Deanna, your mother stole Rustler. I suspect she's going to sell him, if she hasn't already."

Deanna's eyes blazed with indignation. "Don't be ridiculous. You have no right to insult her like that!"

Helen raised her head, but didn't look Deanna in the eye.

"Mom, tell him he's crazy!"

It seemed an eternity before Helen answered. "He's telling the truth. I took Rustler."

Deanna was numb. "You did? *You?*"

Helen nodded miserably.

"But...but why, Mom?"

"Oh, Deanna! Because it was worth it! Because selling him would give us the money we need to pay off our debts and finally put an end to this nonsense."

Appalled, Deanna took a step backward. She would have fallen down the porch steps if J.D. hadn't caught her and pulled her close.

"Tell me this is a joke," Deanna whispered, glad of J.D.'s support. "Come on, Mom. This isn't funny."

"It's no joke. Wake up, Deanna," Helen said angrily. "You had a solution to our problems fall into your hands, but refused to do anything about it."

"But he was my horse! Mine! He wasn't yours to sell."

Helen rose to her feet. "Maybe not, but I'm still glad I did! It's not like Rustler was your child, or a pet lap dog. He's a valuable Thoroughbred. He barely got the attention he needed from you, because you were too busy working to pay off your father's debts!"

Deanna gave J.D. a furtive glance. "Please, Mom! Don't say anything else."

"I know about your mother's probation and your arrangement with the courts, Deanna," J.D. said gently. "I found out about it soon after we first met."

"Who told you?"

"No one told me. I made a point of finding out. Remember? I told you I'd look into your father's dealings with me. I investigated his background—quite thoroughly."

Deanna stared at J.D. and then her mother, unable to believe what she was hearing, yet knowing she had to try to make some sense of it all. J.D. knew about their debts? Helen had sold Rustler?

"Mom, you had no right to take Rustler! He was mine. I was the one who nursed him and took care of him."

"And I was the one who *tried* to take care of you. Only I was weak. I didn't want to go to jail, and I let you suffer for it. Deanna, can't you understand? I let you down! You have no money, no husband, no children, no *life!* I tried to convince you to sell Rustler to Mr. Vaughn. I knew he'd be a good owner, but you were so stubborn."

Deanna wanted to cover her ears with her hands. She wanted to scream. She wanted to throw things. But she could only stand and listen in mute anguish.

"So I waited until you left for the trail ride, and then formed a plan. I knew you'd stop in Tucson to transport the horses. And you and Mr. Vaughn made it easy for me at that gas station. But I was nervous, and I botched things. I forgot to check the gas tank and ended up phoning the police to tell them about the horses." Helen wiped away the tears now falling down her cheeks. "But I got it right the second time. I borrowed a horse, rode out into the desert and waited."

"You, Mom? You rode out alone?"

"Don't look so surprised. Don't forget who taught you how to ride and how to navigate in the desert. When Kathy's son was hurt and you were gone, I took Rustler."

"Where is he?"

Helen shook her head. "Gone. Thanks to the power of attorney you gave me when you left."

Deanna brought a fist up to her mouth. The power of attorney—the one Deanna always made out when she left town. Helen had taken advantage of that? Deanna had to cancel it immediately! If only it wasn't the weekend ...

"You sold him already? Where's the money, Mom? What did you do with it? I want to find the new owner and get Rustler back. This was a fraudulent sale!"

"It wasn't, and you can't. I hired a special courier to pay back every cent to the courts. I even made certain the bank processed my cashier's check right away." She paused. "And I'll pay you what Rustler was worth if it takes me the rest of my life," Helen promised. "You can buy a new horse."

"It isn't just the horse, Mom! I trusted you! And you lied to me!" Deanna's breath came in ragged gasps. "I can't believe you did this. I can't believe this is happening! Where's my copy of the bill of sale?"

Only concrete evidence would convince her this nightmare was real.

"It'll come in the mail in a day or two. So will the court statement. Believe me, Deanna, there's no way you can reverse the sale. It was all legal. Rustler's gone," she repeated firmly.

"Legal? You stole from me—your own daughter—and you call it legal? How could you?"

Helen lifted her chin. "I know you're angry, Deanna. I know you may never forgive me. But at least I'll be able to sleep nights now. I've done what I should have done a long time ago—given you back your life."

She reached out for her daughter, but Deanna jerked away from the outstretched hand. Helen's face crumpled, and she ran into the apartment.

Deanna started shaking. J.D. tried to pull her close, but Deanna pushed him away. "You *knew* my mother stole Rustler! You knew all along, and you never said anything!"

J.D.'s eyes were full of compassion. "I wasn't sure, sweetheart. I prayed I was wrong, but it was the only solution that made sense. The way the horses had been fed and watered before being abandoned outside Tucson. The way your mother was never here when you tried to call her. The way the thief was always one step ahead of us, knowing where we'd be. And the way Helen worried about you ..."

"So you know our whole sad story?" Deanna's expression was hard and accusing. "You knew about our situation all along, and you didn't tell me? No wonder you were so certain I'd sell," she said bitterly. "And so very worried when Rustler was stolen."

J.D. flinched at her words, but his tone was low when he spoke. "That's not true. I'd hoped you'd tell me yourself. I had some foolish idea you might actually ask for my help."

Deanna shook her head, too distressed to hear the ragged edge in his voice.

"I know you're upset, but believe me, I'm on your side. I didn't want to hurt you. I almost didn't tell you about Helen and Rustler, but..." J.D. held his palms up in appeal. "Good Lord, Deanna, what other choice did I have?"

She lifted wet sad eyes to his and saw that his face mirrored her pain. She buried her own face in her hands. This time when he took her in his arms, she didn't resist.

After a long while she raised her head from his chest. The anger was gone, but the ache in her heart remained. She'd trusted her mother and been deceived. She hadn't trusted J.D. and had been proved wrong. The only comfort in all this was the certain knowledge that J. D. Vaughn wasn't the horse thief, after all.

"What will you do now?" he asked her.

Deanna pushed her hair back from her face. "I don't know. Put my tack away. Take a shower. Go to bed. Think."

"Would you like me to stay?"

"No. This is between my mother and me."

"If you're sure..."

Deanna nodded.

"I'll go get your saddle out of the trunk. Where do you want it?"

"In the barn's good."

Deanna watched from the porch swing as J.D. took care of her gear, then returned.

"I'm going to stay in Cactus Gulch for the night," he told her. "If you need me, call the motel, okay?"

"I'll be fine," she said, but neither of them really believed that.

"I'll stop by in the morning before I go home." He bent and kissed her on the cheek. "I know things seem bleak right now. But remember, your mother loves you."

Deanna remained silent. J.D. touched her shoulder, and after a moment her hand crept up to cover his.

"You'd best be going. It'll be dark soon." She awkwardly released his hand, feeling miserable, ashamed and very stupid. "I guess I owe you an apology for all those things I—"

J.D. refused to let her continue. "Don't worry about that, Deanna. Just get some sleep."

"I'll try," she promised, although she doubted she would. "And J.D.?"

"Yes?"

"Thanks. For everything."

She sat on the swing after he'd driven off, unwilling to confront her mother, yet knowing she couldn't stay outside all night. What could they possibly say to one another now?

Hoping her mother had gone to bed, Deanna finally ventured into the apartment. Her heart sank when she saw that Helen had waited up after all.

"Are you hungry?" Helen stood up and gave her a tentative smile. "I fixed you some dinner."

Deanna stared at her. "After everything that's happened, you can talk about food?"

"Maybe you'd like to clean up first? I could run you a bath."

"A bath? You stole my horse, and you want to run me a bath?"

"Deanna, don't," Helen begged. "Please, let's talk."

"What do you want me to say? That it's okay? That I forgive you?"

"I... I can't expect that. But I hoped you'd understand."

"Oh, I understand, all right," Deanna said bitterly. "I understand you value honesty about as much as Dad did."

Deanna regretted the words the second they left her lips, but it was too late to take them back.

"I'm going to bed," she said in the awful silence.

But after a few moments her mother spoke tearfully, "Deanna, I love you."

Deanna shook her head and walked into the bedroom, shutting the door on her mother.

And for the first time in her life, she locked it.

CHAPTER TEN

RUSTLER'S GONE. Mom sold him. Those were Deanna's first thoughts when she awoke late the next morning. Depression settled on her like dust in a barn, but she forced herself to get out of bed. She wondered if some coffee would help, and padded into the kitchen, glad of the time alone.

Helen was at the clinic. As Deanna wasn't supposed to be back from the charity drive yet, the substitute vet, Silas Parker, was still on duty. Deanna supposed she could have relieved him, but he was a retired vet who enjoyed getting his hands back in the business occasionally.

Deanna doubted she'd be much good to her patients, anyway. And the last thing she wanted was to be around Helen.

Mom, how could you? Deanna shook her head and went to make the coffee. It was then that she saw the note. Reluctantly she opened it. "Dear Deanna," it began, "I hope you slept well. I know you probably don't want to see me, but we have to talk. I need to tell you about Rustler's new owner. I'll be home for lunch. Please wait for me." It was signed, "Love, Mother."

Deanna crumpled the note and threw it savagely on the floor. Then, ashamed of herself, she picked it up and threw it in the trash.

I wish J.D. was here. She looked at her watch and saw it was close to eleven o'clock. The poor guy was probably still in bed. Thanks to the Leightons, he hadn't had much sleep lately, either.

Despite her heartache, Deanna smiled at the thought of him. At last she knew she could trust him, knew she was finally free to love him. And he'd promised to come and see her today.

The coffeepot was perking when Deanna heard the sound of a car coming up the driveway. She raced outside and down the steps, smiling widely at the sight of J.D. The smile died as she saw his grim expression.

"J.D.? What's wrong?" she asked, hurrying to his side.

He came straight to the point. "It's about Rustler. Let's go inside and talk."

"Can't we talk about it here? Tell me about my horse. Is he all right? Did you find his new owner?"

"I found both. Rustler's fine."

Deanna let out a sigh of relief and allowed J.D. to direct her up the steps to the porch swing. They both sat.

"Where is he?"

"He's..." J.D. hesitated, something Deanna had never seen him do before. "He's at my ranch, Deanna."

Deanna looked at J.D.'s face. Time froze, and so did her heart. She didn't know how long she stared at him, unable to speak.

Finally J.D. broke the silence. "Your mother offered to sell Rustler to me last night, Deanna."

"I don't understand," she said slowly. "Mom told me she'd already sold him."

"She hadn't, Deanna. She lied because she was afraid you'd stop her." J.D. gazed at her levelly. "She came to the motel after you'd gone to bed and offered him to me. She said that if I didn't take him, she'd sell him to someone else."

Deanna couldn't bring herself to ask the next question. *Did you buy him, J.D.?* She was too afraid to hear the answer.

"I bought Rustler, Deanna. I paid your mother with a bank draft, and she gave me the bill of sale."

Deanna wanted to scream, to rant and rave at his words. But she couldn't. She was paralyzed. The betrayal she'd felt over her mother's actions was nothing like what she was feeling now. She knew J.D.'s eyes were on her and refused to meet his gaze. There was a long moment of silence, then he put a hand on her arm. Still she couldn't look at him.

"Deanna, your mother wouldn't tell me where she'd hidden the power of attorney. It's valid for another three days—until the day the trail ride would have ended. It's the weekend now. You couldn't have canceled it before Monday. If I didn't buy him, Helen would have found someone else who would!"

"How convenient that you showed up, then," Deanna managed to say. She'd been so stupid, so trusting. Last night while she was suffering, J.D. had been busy cheating her. She'd fallen for his phony lines just like her father had.

"Deanna?" J.D.'s voice was hoarse and urgent. "Deanna!" He shook her arm, hard. "Tell me you understand."

"Understand?" That word shocked Deanna out of her numbness. "What's to understand? It's pretty obvious, wouldn't you say? You could have come back and told me. I could have called my lawyer at home and found a way to cancel that power of attorney. Instead, you just bought Rustler." She flung herself out of the swing, away from his touch.

J.D. followed her to the far end of the porch. "Deanna, I only bought Rustler to keep him safe! Your mother was desperate! She would have sold him to anyone! I didn't want him to end up in the wrong hands. He's already had one abusive owner."

"How noble of you," Deanna said bitterly, deliberately turning her back on him. "Am I supposed to be grateful?"

"I bought him for *you,* not for *me!*"

Deanna whirled around to face him again, her face deathly white. "You expect me to believe that? How stupid do you think I am?" *Stupid enough to let you hurt me like this,* her heart cried. "But then I guess you figured, like father, like daughter, right? We Leightons are such easy marks."

"Sweetheart, please! I did it for us!" He reached for her, but Deanna batted his hand away.

"Us? *Us?* Don't make me laugh. Poor Rustler never had a chance. And neither did I!" All Deanna's hopes and dreams for a life with J.D. died. "I finally trusted you! Do you know I was even falling in love with you? What a joke!"

The desperation left his face, replaced by anger and another fierce emotion she couldn't quite identify. "It's no joke, Deanna. It means a great deal to me."

"I'll bet it does. I'll bet you had a good laugh every time you kissed me. When all you wanted was the damn horse."

"You're wrong!"

"I'm not." She blinked back tears. She would *not* cry in front of him. "Well, I hope you'll be very happy racing Rustler. Maybe you can hire my mother to help you. The two of you make a good team."

J.D. grabbed her and pulled her into an embrace. "I swear to you, Deanna, I bought the horse for you and only you. No other reason. You can have him back. I *want* to give him back, just as soon as that power of attorney you gave your mother expires."

Deanna wrenched away from his grasp. "If Mom has the money, I'm sure it's all gone now. Even if it isn't, there's no way she's going to give it to me. Don't you understand? I can't return your money."

"To hell with the money! I don't want it."

"Well, I don't want your charity. And I don't want you."

J.D.'s face blanched. "You . . . you can't mean that."

"I do. You have Rustler," Deanna said in a hollow voice. "So please go."

"I don't care about Rustler! I care about *you!* Deanna, I love you!"

The three words she once would have rejoiced to hear meant nothing now. "I don't believe you, J.D. Not now." She met his eyes dispassionately.

The two of them stared at one another in silence. Then Deanna heard a truck pull up. It was Helen, home for lunch.

"Maybe your mother can talk some sense into you," J.D. said bitterly. "I told her I was buying the horse for you. If you don't believe *me*, maybe you'll believe *her.*"

"Talking to my mother is the last thing I need!" But apparently J.D. had made up his mind, allowing her no say in the matter. He blocked her path, forcing Deanna to wait until Helen joined them.

"Darling, I just got back from the courthouse. We're free and clear. And your horse has the best home possible," Helen said eagerly.

"So I've heard." Deanna could barely get the words out.

Helen nervously glanced from her to J.D. "Oh, you know. Well, J.D. will take good care of Rustler. He'll take good care of you, too, if you'd let him."

"Let him take care of me?" Deanna was incredulous. "I don't trust him any more that I trust you." She turned and started down the steps.

"Deanna? Deanna, where are you going?" Helen asked.

And then, as Deanna hurried into the truck Helen had vacated, she heard J.D.'s hoarse, "Deanna, come back!"

Deanna pulled her keys out her jeans pocket and started the engine. She had to get away before she heard one more lie. She didn't look back, not even when Helen frantically called her name or J.D. dashed to his own car to follow her.

She deliberately headed for Cactus Gulch's back roads, driving far into the desert. J.D.'s fancy car couldn't follow her there. And when her truck could no longer handle the rugged landscape, either, she simply laid her forehead down on the steering wheel . . . and cried.

WHEN HER TEARS finally stopped, she was as dry as the desert itself—and inside, just as barren and desolate. But by then she was ready to face reality and admit to herself that she'd made mistakes.

She'd trusted J. D. Vaughn, only to be cheated out of her horse—and her heart. At least Helen had Deanna's interests at heart when she sold Rustler, no matter how misguided she was. But J.D.'s sole motive for his coldhearted lies was monetary gain.

He was waiting for her on the porch when she finally returned home hours later. His calm logical sentences changed to impassioned pleas as he tried to explain things. When Deanna still refused to respond, he exploded.

"Why can't you see reason?" he yelled. "I'm not the bad guy here!"

But she remained unmoved. "You've got what you wanted," she told him impassively. "I don't ever want to see you again."

Eventually he left. And he didn't come back. Not that day, nor in the days that followed.

"I knew he was bad news the first time he showed up here," Deanna said to her mother at work weeks later. "I hope he treats horses better than he treats women, or Rustler's going to have a miserable life."

Mother and daughter were speaking again. Deanna had come to accept her mother's actions. It had been Kathy who'd helped her to see reason.

"You don't have children, Deanna," she'd said. "You can't possibly understand what a mother will do to protect her child. I know I'd go to the ends of the earth for Shawn." Kathy had patted Deanna's cheek. "You don't have to condone what she did. But try to understand—and forgive."

And finally Deanna had. She'd extended a tentative olive branch, and Helen had tearfully accepted it. Deanna refused to let Helen pay her back for Rustler. "I think we've wasted enough time in debt. Just forget about the money."

"Can you forget about it, Deanna? Can you ever forgive me for what I've done? You don't laugh anymore. You don't even smile. I hate seeing you like this."

"I just need time," Deanna replied, but her words didn't convince Helen.

"First, I ruined things with Rustler, then I ruined them with J.D. He told me he was only buying the horse for you, not for his ranch."

Deanna could have screamed. Somehow J.D. had managed to successfully con three Leightons. "He only said that so you'd sell Rustler to him," she said through gritted teeth. "Surely you don't believe he was serious."

"I do! Won't you talk to him? Deanna, J.D. loves you!"

Deanna's expression turned hard. "If you ever want our relationship to be the way it was before, Mother, you'll never mention that man's name to me again. Do you understand?"

A sorrowful Helen had no choice but to agree.

So the days passed with monotonous regularity, one after another. Deanna stayed busy. Since the money from her practice wasn't going to the courts, she was able to make improvements both at home and around the clinic. New clothes for her mother were a priority, along with pristine tile to replace the ancient linoleum in her office. She even splurged on a new coat of paint for the exterior. Deanna also hired someone to take care of the heavy cleaning, permanently freeing her and Helen from the tedious chore. But anything beyond that didn't interest her.

"Deanna, aren't you going to buy anything for yourself?" Helen asked. "I feel guilty spending all this money on just me."

"I don't want anything," she replied dispiritedly. *Except J.D.*

And he was the one thing Deanna couldn't have.

Finally Helen went out shopping for Deanna herself. "Early birthday presents, darling," she said gaily.

Deanna found herself surrounded by clothes and trinkets and all the pretty things she'd denied herself for so long. Only now she had no desire for them. Who would she wear them for? Her patients? But for Helen's sake, she graciously accepted the gifts. Helen even adopted a greyhound for Deanna and presented the animal with a big pink bow.

"Her name is Belle. I know she's not Rustler," Helen said with a tremor in her voice, "but she's very affectionate and quite calm. She'll be good company for you.

"Thanks, Mom." The dog tentatively licked Deanna's hand. Deanna fondled the delicate ears and was rewarded with another wet kiss. "She's lovely."

"Oh, and there's one last gift. You pawned all your nice things, so I thought you should have this."

Deanna opened a brightly wrapped box, and found a blue-and-silver necklace and matching earrings.

"Do you like it? Turquoise is your birthstone, you know."

Deanna was aghast to find tears filling her eyes. All she could hear was J.D. talking about receiving his turquoise pieces from his sister. And she didn't need another reminder of him.

"I don't want them, Mom," Deanna said, gruffly shoving the box into her mother's hands. "Please take them back."

And so Helen returned them, wisely asking no questions.

The only time Deanna saw J.D. now was in her dreams, where he gazed at her, accusing and reproachful.

"Why can't I just forget about him?" she cried to her mother. It was late on a Sunday night—the night Deanna had finally accepted that J.D. was gone from her life forever.

"Maybe because you love him."

"No, I don't," Deanna said with a lump in her throat. She sat cross-legged on the porch swing, Belle curled at her feet. "There can't be love without trust. And I can't trust him. J.D. was as guilty as sin when it came to cheating me out of Rustler."

Helen sighed. "No, Deanna. I was the only guilty party where Rustler was concerned." She sat down next to Deanna, and continued, "I remember when I was in court. I knew I was innocent. All during the trial I was confident that the jury would believe me. I was shattered when they didn't. You've done the same thing to J.D. that they did to me."

Deanna closed her eyes. "I wasn't wrong," she whispered. "If he was so innocent, why isn't he here? Why haven't I heard from him?"

"Darling, the man offered you his love, and you threw it back in his face! You wouldn't even listen to his side of the story. So he left. What did you expect him to do?"

"He could have at least tried again!"

"We all have our limits, Deanna. Even strong men like him." Helen rose from the swing. "No one knows that better than me."

Deanna let her mother leave without protest. Could Helen be right? Had she foolishly thrown away her chance at happiness? Had pain and pride blinded her to the truth?

All she really knew was that she missed J.D. desperately—so desperately that she tried to convince herself that his guilt didn't matter. But it did. There was no way around it.

One sleepless night Deanna forced herself to think calmly about what had happened. She'd been hoping and praying for J.D. to appear again. The short time she'd known him had changed her life irrevocably. He'd shown her what it meant to live, instead of just exist. She remembered the first kiss they'd shared and the ones that had followed. She remembered his white face when she'd been trapped beneath Rustler and how he'd come back for her, instead of going after the thief. And she remembered how he'd taken her back to the wagon train nurse before looking twice at Rustler.

And then, with a guilty flush, she remembered how he'd looked when she'd sent him away.

Suddenly Deanna was ashamed of herself. Ashamed and disappointed. She'd forgiven her mother, but she'd hurt an innocent man—a man she dearly loved. In her heart she'd believed in J. D. Vaughn, but she'd simply refused to listen to her heart because of her father's betrayal. And now she'd thrown away something precious—not because of Rustler, but because she was afraid of being betrayed again.

J.D. hadn't deceived Deanna any more than he'd deceived Carl. No, like her father, Deanna had simply deceived herself.

If she had the courage, she'd find him and face him again. She now knew she'd been wrong. J.D. deserved an apology.

But Deanna was afraid—afraid that she'd been too foolish, afraid that she'd waited too long. And so she did nothing, unwilling to go to J.D. in case he told her he didn't want her foolish self anymore.

Until one Monday morning brought her more heartache.

"Deanna, I think you'd better open this," Helen said slowly. They were at the clinic, taking a break for lunch.

Deanna was immediately on guard. Helen usually opened all the mail for her. "What is it?"

"Here." Helen held out a large manila envelope. "It's from the Rocking J Ranch."

Deanna saw J.D.'s bold scrawl across the front. Her hand was shaking as she took the envelope from Helen.

"Shall I leave you alone?"

"No. I'm fine." Only she wasn't; her heart was pounding and she couldn't breathe.

"Maybe there's a letter inside," her mother said. "Open it."

Deanna did. Her heart sank as her hands touched something soft. "There's no letter, Mom." Her eyes closed in pain.

"Then what...?"

Deanna shook her head. She knew what she'd see when she opened her eyes: a blue cloth bandanna—J.D.'s final farewell. Deanna closed the envelope, rethreading the little metal hook through the hole with trembling fingers. Helen said nothing as Deanna pushed her lunch aside and left the room.

In her office, Deanna forced herself to take the blue bandanna out of the envelope. She gently ran the material through her fingers, ashamed of herself for hiding. It was time to prove she was no coward. It was time to fight for what she wanted.

Helen politely knocked, then opened the door to the office a crack. "Deanna? It's almost time to open up again. Are you ready?"

"We aren't opening."

"We're not?"

"No, because I'm not going to be here. Call Silas Parker and see if he'll fill in for me."

"But Deanna, we have a full schedule this afternoon!" Helen called out as Deanna reached for her purse and truck keys. "Where are you going?"

"To see a man about a horse!"

CHAPTER ELEVEN

DEANNA'S TRUCK covered the cracked desert pavement in record time. She only slowed after she drove under the sign proudly proclaiming the entrance to the Rocking J.

"Your name?" the security guard asked at the gate.

"Deanna Leighton. I'm here to see Mr. Vaughn."

The guard checked his book. "I don't see your name listed here in his appointment book, miss. I'm afraid I'll have to check with the main office."

"Sorry, I can't wait. I'll check myself." Deanna stepped on the accelerator. So much for security, Deanna thought as she sped down the paved drive. Another security man was waiting for her.

"I'd like to see Mr. Vaughn, please," she told him as she got out of her truck. "Tell him Dr. Leighton from Cactus Gulch is here." On the outside, she was boldly assertive. Inside, she was shaking. What if J.D. refused to see her?

Please, J.D., please, she begged silently. *Give me another chance.*

She bit her lip as the guard did as she asked, then prayed like she'd never prayed before.

Suddenly he was there. The face was haggard, thinner than she remembered, and his stance didn't seem as assured as usual, but it was still J.D.

The man she trusted. The man she loved.

Deanna looked up into his eyes and felt her nerve fail at his forbidding expression—but only for a moment.

"Could we go into your office, please?" she asked. "We need to talk."

He said nothing, but nodded his head and gestured for her to follow. He led her inside and took the chair behind the desk once Deanna was settled in the one before it.

"Well?"

Deanna hated hearing the coldness his voice. This wasn't going to be easy. But then, nothing in life worth fighting for ever was. She straightened her shoulders.

"I came here to apologize." To her dismay, the words didn't seem to affect him. There was no softening of his features. "I should never have accused you of..."

"Lying? Cheating? Outright theft?" he angrily supplied.

Deanna's cheeks burned with guilt. "You've done none of those things. I was wrong. I believe you've been honest and aboveboard since the day I met you."

J.D. crossed his arms, his eyes narrowed and unreadable. "Tell me. How did this sudden revelation come about? Did your mother twist your arm and force you to come here?"

"No. Coming here was my idea. It's been a while since the trail ride...." Four weeks and five days, to be exact. She knew; she'd counted. "And I've had time to think things through. You know, make some sense of it all."

J.D. gave her a disdainful look. "You always were short on sense when it came to Rustler. Or me."

Deanna couldn't deny that. Nor could she deny that this visit wasn't going as planned. J.D. didn't look happy to see her at all.

"So, Dr. Leighton?"

And now she wasn't even Deanna to him anymore. Her heart sank. "So, I'm sorry. Really and truly sorry."

"Apology accepted. Was there anything else?"

"No, I guess that's about it."

"You're sure?"

Deanna nodded, the disdain in his voice making her feel worse.

"Don't you want to see Rustler?"

She did want to see her horse—her former horse—but refused to succumb to the temptation. "It's probably better for Rustler that I stay away. I don't want to interfere with his adjustment to a new home."

"You won't even check on your own horse?" he asked incredulously.

"But . . . Rustler's yours!"

Her reply seemed to anger J.D. further. "I *told* you I bought Rustler for you! I thought that was why you were here—to pick him up."

"To pick him up?" she echoed. Her surprise was genuine, and so was J.D.'s fury.

"So you still don't trust me." He sprang out of his chair and turned to stare out through the huge window.

"I never said that!"

J.D. whirled to face her. "Didn't you? You come here with your pretty little apology, but you still don't believe anything I've said!"

"I do! I believe you dealt with my father as honestly as you have with me!" she insisted, standing up herself.

"Then you might as well have the proof. That's what you really want, isn't it?" J.D. reached into a desk drawer and snatched out a folder, which he flung at her. Confused, Deanna hesitated.

"Go on, read it."

She cautiously did as he ordered. There, along with Rustler's Arizona horse registration and bloodline papers, was a notarized bill of sale for Rustler to Deanna Leighton for the sum of one dollar. Deanna turned pale when she saw the date on the paperwork. It was the day after Helen's power of attorney had expired.

Just as J.D. promised.

Still holding the bill in her hand, her eyes met his.

"You never really believed me, did you? You actually thought I meant to keep him all along." He continued to stand at the window. The tense anger was gone from his body and voice. Only weary resignation remained—and a pain Deanna was determined to erase.

"I never thought about getting Rustler back," she insisted. In truth, she hadn't. Rustler's loss had been nothing compared to the loss of J.D.

"You expect me to believe that?"

"Yes!"

"You just said you thought things through! In all this time, don't tell me you forgot about the damn horse!"

"That's right. I thought about you. Only you."

A strange emotion flickered in his eyes. "And not Rustler?"

"Not about getting him back, no."

The strange emotion vanished. "Now you're the one who's lying. Since the day I met you, all you ever cared about was Rustler—and who wanted to buy him, or steal him, or own him."

"So I had my priorities wrong, I admit it," she announced. "I should have been concentrating on us."

"Us? Now that's a joke. There is no *us*. The only couple around here is you and Rustler."

"I want us, you and I, to have a future together," Deanna said boldly. "A life together."

J.D. shook his head. "I don't know whether to believe you or not. Even if I did, you're too late."

"J.D., I love you! It's never too late!"

"Considering you didn't bother telling me until *after* you saw the bill of sale, I'd say it is."

Deanna swayed at the finality in his words. For a dizzying moment, she thought she was going to faint. She leaned forward and grabbed the desk as she damned her stupid pride and unlucky timing. She should have blurted out her feelings for him the moment she saw him! Now she had *his* stupid pride to deal with!

"I'll get one of the guards to help you to your truck," J.D. offered after a mortifying silence. He remained at the window, the desk a barrier between them, but not as big a barrier as the expression on his face.

"No, thank you," she said with what dignity she could muster. "I'll be just fine."

"You probably will." J.D. didn't bother to hide the sarcasm. "Goodbye, Deanna. And don't forget this." He threw her Rustler's file. "I wouldn't want to be accused of unfair business practices. *Again.*"

Deanna picked it up. She pulled out the bill of sale and dropped the rest of the papers on the desk.

"Give me your pen so I can sign Rustler back over to you."

"How very noble, Deanna, but you don't fool me."

"Are you calling me a liar?" Deanna gasped. He actually thought she was bluffing!

J.D.'s lip curled in disdain. "You'd die before you'd give up your precious horse."

"You're wrong. You mean more to me than anything. Certainly more than Rustler." And before J.D.'s shocked gaze, she deliberately shredded the bill of sale into tiny pieces, then threw them at him with the same violence he'd thrown Rustler's file at her.

"He's yours, J.D. What do you think of *that?*"

Not a word came from him. No hint of emotion showed in his face. J.D. just stood like a statue while Deanna died a thousand deaths inside. Finally she knew it was time to leave, but she'd be damned if she'd leave his office without one last word.

"I hope Rustler's trophies will keep you warm at night," she said, then spun on her heel and left. Even as she made her way to the truck, even as she told herself he was a bigger fool than she was, Deanna was listening for him, waiting to hear a footstep or him calling her name.

She slowed her pace. Still nothing. Even when she started the truck and loudly revved the engine so he'd hear her—nothing. Deanna fought the tears and pulled out of the parking lot. Obviously winning J.D.'s trust was going to be harder than she thought. But she refused to think that it was impossible.

They'd already wasted so much time. All because of pride. She was positive he loved her, but she wasn't as sure that he'd unbend enough to tell her. At least, not today. She'd return tomorrow, she vowed. She wasn't giving up.

She swiped at her damp cheeks and continued to drive. She might as well head over to the clinic, after all, since she didn't know if Silas had been able to take over.

The brood mares in the field she was passing neighed and scattered. Deanna immediately checked her speed. She didn't think she was going fast enough to frighten them, but there was no sense in disturbing gestating mares unnecessarily.

The mares continued to act spooked, and Deanna searched for the reason. She looked in her rearview mirror. What she saw had her foot slamming on the brakes. Behind her was a horse and rider. The horse wasn't familiar, but the rider certainly was. It was J.D., and he was galloping along beside the fence that separated the field from the road.

Her heart gave a leap. Was it possible? Could he be coming after her?

"Deanna? Deanna, wait!"

She immediately turned off the ignition and flew out of the truck.

"Deanna," he repeated breathlessly as he caught up to her. "Don't go."

Hope dared to raise its rainbow hues. "You don't hate me?"

"Oh, no. Not even when I tried, I couldn't. Deanna, please don't leave me again."

His love was on his face, and the truth was in his eyes.

"I won't," she said.

He dismounted, not even bothering to secure his horse. Instead, he vaulted over the fence and hauled her close. "You don't believe I tried to sweet-talk you out of Rustler?"

"No."

"You believe I bought Rustler to give him back to you?"

"Yes."

His face filled with wonder, and he gently cupped her face with his hands. "You don't regret destroying that bill of sale?"

"Oh, J.D., no! I love you! "

If she could convince a hard-hearted judge to keep her mother out of jail, surely she could convince one big-hearted man she meant every word. "I've been such a fool! I'd trust you with my horse, my heart, my life. Can't you believe me?"

He sighed, wrapping her in his arms once more and pulling her tight against his chest. "I needed to hear that so much," he whispered. "When you tore up the bill of sale, I think I went into shock. I'd hoped—waited for you to come after me for so long."

"Like you just came after me."

"You bet I did. You're never getting away from me again." J.D. pressed his mouth to hers to seal his vow. "I love you, Deanna Leighton. You *are* going to marry me?" he asked between frantic kisses.

"Yes."

"And we're going to live happily ever after?"

"Yes."

J.D. stopped kissing her to gaze into her eyes. "Despite what happened to your father?"

"Despite what happened to my father. His problems were of his own making, J.D., not yours. I know that now. My heart has always known it, even if my head didn't."

"It took you long enough!" He then proceeded to kiss her again. Soon they had a curious audience of ranch hands, brood mares, security guards and one riderless mount.

"Maybe you should retrieve your horse," Deanna murmured between kisses. "And I should get my truck out of the middle of the road. We're becoming quite the attraction."

"Later."

"But—"

"It's my ranch, my horse and my road. They can wait. This can't." J.D. kissed her again. He ignored the whistling and catcalls from the human spectators, but an embarrassed Deanna could not.

"J.D.," she whispered against his mouth, "aren't you going to make them stop?"

He lifted his lips from hers and smiled wickedly.

"J.D.," Deanna weakly protested, her body afire with his touch. "They're all watching. Do something! Anything!"

At those words he lowered his mouth to hers again and did something—very, very thoroughly.

EPILOGUE

THE LAST NOTES of "My Old Kentucky Home" faded away, and the huge crowd at the annual running of the Kentucky Derby cheered their approval. The trumpet sounded the post parade of the horses.

From their box, Mr. and Mrs. J. D. Vaughn, owners of the Derby favorite, watched the racing silks of the Rocking J Ranch flutter by.

"Come on, Rustler! You can do it!" Deanna yelled as the horse and rider left the paddock and headed toward the track.

J.D. laughed. "Are you certain Rustler can hear you in this crowd?"

"Of course he can. It doesn't matter how many jockeys you stick up on him, he still likes me best."

J.D. pulled her close for a quick kiss. "Rustler has very good taste," he murmured.

"I don't care about his taste. I just want him to win," Deanna maintained. "Remember, you told me I could have half the purse if he crosses the finish line first."

Soon after their marriage, Deanna had agreed to let J.D. race Rustler all he wanted, providing Rustler was happy. Not surprisingly, Rustler had lived up to his bloodlines. He'd proved to be a consistent winner as a two-year-old and had established the Rocking J as a Thoroughbred stable to be reckoned with. Some of his prize winnings had helped Deanna establish her new equine veterinary practice in

Phoenix. The rest of the money had gone to animal rights.

Deanna wanted to continue that work and was hoping for even more success now that Rustler was racing as a three-year-old.

"I always keep my promises," J.D. assured her. "Well, what charity gets the money this time? Abused horses? Homeless dogs?" His eyes twinkled. "Battered butterflies?"

"Very funny." Deanna hit him with her racing program, the turquoise bracelet he'd given her gleaming on her wrist. "I'm not giving any of it to my usual charities this time. If Rustler wins—"

"*When* he wins," J.D. corrected. "We racehorse owners are very superstitious."

"When he wins," Deanna amended, giving her husband a loving look. He was wearing her old blue bandanna again, but it was sentiment—not superstition—that prompted its appearance around his neck. He had reclaimed it soon after their engagement, shamelessly admitting he'd returned it as a way of provoking her to visit.

"When he wins, I'm giving most of my share to the children's shelter in downtown Phoenix. Those poor babies..." Deanna's hand spread protectively over the soft material of her maternity top. "It's not just the animals who need our help, J.D."

"I know." J.D.'s hand came to rest over her own. "That was why I gave that check to Matt Caldwell for his special dude ranch. It was a stroke of genius, your asking him to take the check as a special favor to an expectant mother. There was no way he could rip it up and send it back."

"Matt's just like you—a big softie," Deanna insisted. "I don't know why you two fight so much. It must be a male thing. Hormones or something."

J.D. grinned and patted her burgeoning belly. "I've never heard you complain about my hormones before, sweetheart."

Deanna started to hit him with the program again, but found herself being kissed instead. "Stop distracting me, J.D.!" she chastised after he let her go. "I want to watch Rustler."

"You mean you want to watch him win, my greedy little wife. That reminds me. You said you were donating most of your winnings to the children's shelter. What are you going to do for a wedding present for your mother if Rustler doesn't comes through?" he asked.

"Rustler will win. Even if he doesn't, I'm determined to send Mom and Silas to Hawaii for their honeymoon."

"Silas was determined to make Helen his wife. You vets don't know when to give up."

"Thank goodness we don't, or you and I would still be single and fighting over Rustler's ownership."

"I would have come after you sooner or later. I knew a good thing when I saw it." J.D. shook his head. "I still can't believe Silas bought your old practice when you married me. You know, I always wondered why Helen wouldn't come to work for you at your new practice. I thought she hated Cactus Gulch."

"She surprised us all." Deanna squeezed J.D.'s hand. "I'm glad Mom's found someone to make her laugh again. She's so happy now. Like me."

J.D. moved to kiss her once more, but Deanna broke away as the track announcer came over the loudspeakers.

"The horses are now loading...."

"Oh, I can't see Rustler! J.D., where are those binoculars?"

"To hell with the binoculars."

He reached for her and drew her into his arms, ignoring the announcer's, "They're in the starting gate...."

"I want to kiss my wife."

"But the race is about to start! So much is riding on this! I want money for the children's shelter, and I want to send Mom on a nice honeymoon. Besides, Rustler needs to win big to bring more attention to your stables. J.D., there's a lot on the line here!"

J.D. only smiled a superior smile. "I don't *always* concern myself with high stakes." He reached under her chin and gently tilted her head back. "Sometimes, my love, it pays to go for the sure thing."

As the announcer screamed, "They're off!" and J.D.'s lips came down on hers, Deanna happily decided he was right.

Let

HARLEQUIN ROMANCE®

take you

BACK TO THE RANCH

Come to SkyRim Ranch in Bison County, Nebraska!

Meet Abbie Hale, rancher's daughter—a woman who
loves her family ranch and loves the ranching life.
Then meet Yates Connley, the stranger who comes to
SkyRim for Christmas....

Read Bethany Campbell's
The Man Who Came for Christmas,
our next Back to the Ranch title.
Available in December
wherever Harlequin books are sold.

**Fifty red-blooded, white-hot, true-blue hunks
from every State in the Union!**

Look for MEN MADE IN AMERICA! Written by some
of our most poplar authors, these stories feature fifty of
the strongest, sexiest men, each from a different state in
the union!

Two titles available every other month at your favorite
retail outlet.

In November, look for:

STRAIGHT FROM THE HEART by Barbara Delinsky
(Connecticut)
AUTHOR'S CHOICE by Elizabeth August (Delaware)

In January, look for:

DREAM COME TRUE by Ann Major (Florida)
WAY OF THE WILLOW by Linda Shaw (Georgia)

You won't be able to resist MEN MADE IN AMERICA!

Make Christmas a truly
Romantic experience—with

◈ HARLEQUIN ROMANCE®

Wouldn't *you* love to kiss a tall, dark
Texan under the mistletoe? Gwen does,
in HOME FOR CHRISTMAS by
Ellen James. Share the experience!

Wouldn't *you* love to kiss a sexy
New Englander on a snowy Christmas
morning? Angela does, in Shannon
Waverly's CHRISTMAS ANGEL.
Share the experience!

Look for both of these Christmas
Romance titles, available in December
wherever Harlequin Books are sold.

(And don't forget that Romance novels
make great gifts! Easy to buy, easy to
wrap and just the right size for a
stocking stuffer. And they make a
wonderful treat when you need a break
from Christmas shopping, Christmas
wrapping and stuffing stockings!)

HRXT